Veiled Allurement

A CINDERELLA RETELLING NOVELLA

BY

Elle Beaumont

VEILED ALLUREMENT
Copyright © 2018 by Elle Beaumont.

Published by Crescent Sea Publishing.
www.crescentseapublishing.com

Cover designed by Reading Transforms.
Image copyright © K.M. Robinson Photography.

Kendel,
you'll always be my Prince Charming.

Faye awoke with a start—the sound of chirping birds deafened her as she groped at the ground and tried to gather her wits. All that met her hands was a fistful of pine needles, and as she opened her eyes, blackness met her.

Panic filled her as she stumbled back and landed on her bottom, hands flailing to grasp at something—anything.

With a splash, her hands landed in the icy water. She gasped and lifted a hand in front of her face but saw nothing.

"What—what has happened?" she cried out and hurriedly reached toward her face with shaking hands. She felt it then, a smooth plate covered the majority of her face except for just below her nose.

Terror lanced through her like an arrow. The mask, the fact she was here, it was a cruel joke—it had to be!

The mask had no eye sockets, and it clung so tightly to her flesh that no light filtered in through any cracks. She was blinded.

A whimper left her as her fingers attempted to pry it loose, but there was no use it wouldn't budge.

Memories of how it happened seemed just out of her reach, vaguely she recalled her sister threatening her. One would think she would remember something like this, but when she attempted to retrieve the information, a spike of pain throbbed in her skull.

A sob lodged in her throat. How was she even to begin to know where she was if she couldn't see? She clambered forward and began to pat at the ground, knowing she at least needed to find somewhere that had traffic.

When she moved forward, she felt a tug at her person, not her flesh, but the skirt of her dress. She craned her body to untangle the fabric from whatever it was snagged on, except when she went to untangle it there was no tree and no bush.

A furry muzzle tickled Faye's fingertips and fear reared its ugly head again. Just as a snarl escaped the beast, she yanked her hand bank and narrowly missed the snapping teeth.

What it was, she couldn't say, but judging by the growl, she guessed it was a wild dog or wolf.

There was no time to think about it; she lifted her bare foot and kicked in the direction of the beast, connecting with it before she blindly took off running.

Branches slapped against her skin, and rocks cut into her bare feet as she ran blindly through the woods. What was her other option, stop and die?

Mid-stride, Faye's foot hit the air, there was no ground beneath her, and she went tumbling down a hill. She clawed at the ground in an attempt to halt herself and yet found no purchase. It seemed as though she found every blasted rock on the way down, her bare ankle caught a half-rotted stump, which made her yelp in pain.

Eventually, her body came to a stop at the foot of the hill. She lay prone in the middle of a heavily trodden path. Every part of her body ached, but it was her ankle that throbbed angrily.

The wolf moved with lithe grace down the hill, and it didn't hesitate to claim its prize. With its maw opened wide, it went to launch at her.

"Hey! Get on out of here!" a voice called out, spooking the wolf.

It skittered away, snarling.

"What in Etain's name…" A boot landed next to Faye's head.

Disoriented, she began to roll onto her side when she was stilled by a calloused hand on her bare shoulder. She cried out in pain, as she was getting ready to throw a blind punch.

"Don't move, miss. You're in a bad way." His voice was soft.

It was a strange feeling, not being able to see, not knowing where she was or who stood before her, if they were friend or foe. She swallowed roughly and began to reach inwardly toward her abilities.

Nothing. Faye felt nothing. Not an ounce of her prior abilities, there was no calling on the heavens or the earth.

"What's your name, miss?" the younger voice asked.

Her name was on the tip of her tongue, and she wondered how much she should divulge. Opting to remain reasonably truthful, she told the man.

"Faye, my name is Faye."

Her thick hair tumbled to the side, and she heard a sharp intake of breath at the sight of her face or instead what was in place of it.

The man whistled as he heard the name."Okay, Faye, mind me asking why a mask covers your face?" The older man almost chuckled as his rough fingers prodded at the corner of it as if to attempt to pull it off.

"Don't—I mean, you can't. I've tried." Her voice came out cracked from running and breathing hard.

"Nonsense, of course, I can, it's only a mask." Poised to try, the older man lifted a hand.

The younger male stepped forward and tugged him back. "Maybe leave it, we don't know why it's there. Maybe there is a disfiguration, leave it for now, yeah?" he prompted softly.

"All right. Nevertheless, can't leave you here like this. Your dress is in tatters, you've got cuts, and that ankle looks downright mean." He ran his fingers through his short-cropped hair. "Name's Leon, this is Jacob. You landed right in front of our cart, damn near spooked Faith. I'm on my way to deliver some goods, Jacob is bummin' a ride from me." In spite of the fact she had disrupted their journey, he wasn't grumbling, and he began to gather up Faye in his arms.

Pain seared through her body, uncertain if she had broken anything. She hissed and grasped onto his strong arm.

"You're all right, I promise I won't drop ya. Quit looking so squeamish, Jacob. Ain't no other way to make sure she's okay and can't leave her there."

Jacob peeled his thick jacket off, it was winter, and although there was no snow on the ground, the air had a definite bite to it.

Leon placed Faye on top of the jacket. "Thank you," she began and found a warm coat soon encompassing her form.

"It's the right thing to do. Where are you from anyway? You don't look like you're from these parts…" His skin was the color of dusk, as was Jacob's. In comparison, she stuck out like a sore thumb with her alabaster skin.

Alindor would merely have to do for an answer because things were far more complicated. "Kathill, Alindor."

Silence spread between them for a moment and Leon nodded. "Hm, okay. Well, we should get you seen by someone. Ain't no doctor or nothing, but I'd wager you've got some swelling in your noggin'."

"We know a place where they'll take care of you," Jacob reassured her and eyed her ankle. "They might be able to help your ankle."

The road did little to soothe Faye's aches, and it was far bumpier than she would like, considering her previous ordeal. She found that Leon and Jacob were generous companions. Even though the last thing she wanted was a bit of food, they had offered her some as well as drink.

She drank greedily, and it was all that her stomach would currently consider and the fresh water tasted like heaven to her.

"Nearly there." Jacob turned around to look at Faye, inspecting her limb for limb at least what he could see. "You're definitely from Alindor, that is for certain." He spoke more to himself than he did his companions.

In spite of being covered in bruises, scratches, and mud, it was easy to distinguish that Faye had pale skin. Her limbs were bird-like which gave her a frail, girlish appearance, unlike the Melothrian women who were akin to oxen. They were built to endure unforgiving summers, extended harvests and were altogether more hearty than their northern cousins.

"Is that where I am? Alindor?" The name sounded strange on her tongue, something about it didn't agree with her.

"No ma'am," chimed Leon. "We are in Melothra, just south of Alindor's border, Piram to be exact. Technically, I think where we're headin' is right on the line. A few land feuds had gone on there the past few years." He paused for a moment and chuckled.

"The lady who owns the land and the establishment on it refuses to be part of Melothra, says she ain't nothin' like the chicken-hearted Melothrians."

"That doesn't mean it's Alindor," Jacob muttered softly.

"Bah! Symetrics." Leon waved his hand in the air and urged Faith down the pathway.

"You mean semantics?"

"Look at here, Mr. Teacher, I meant what I said. Symetrics." An exasperated puff of breath escaped him.

Faye bit her bottom lip and tried not to laugh at their quarrel. It was difficult to say how young Jacob was, but if he was a teacher, he was at least old enough to have finished schooling. Leon's voice sounded aged with its gruffness.

She pulled the coat around herself tightly, the fur around the neck tickled her skin, but it was a pleasant sensation. Between the swaying of the carriage and the feeling of the coat, it was almost enough to cause her to slip into another slumber.

Just as she began to doze off, the thunderous voice of Leon roused her.

"Here!" His hand clapped against his leg as he stood up and eyed Jacob.

Jacob looked as startled as Faye, except his face was a mixture of surprise and a scowl.

Where here was, she hadn't the foggiest idea because everything was fog at this point. Not a thin film, but the kind that felt like—well, like a mask.

The house seemed somewhat out of place in the middle of the woods, and it had two stories which happened to be an uncommon thing for a cabin in the middle of nowhere. A large porch with a neat pile of wood in the corner and next to it a rocking chair.

There was a barn somewhere in the back, that much Faye discerned. She heard the chickens clucking and a goat bleating. Amidst the pine scent, there was also the distinct smell of livestock, nothing foul, but earthy.

"No, I'll get her." Leon waved Jacob off and climbed into the back of the cart where the goods were. Toned arms slipped around her lithe figure again and scooped her up. "Careful, don't move too much."

The door to the two-story establishment opened and out came a middle-aged woman with wavy, white hair. "Leon, so good to see you, what have you there?" She motioned to the battered female.

A wry smile passed over Leon's face. "You know me, always pickin' up the strays. Found him and her on the trail." He jerked his chin toward Jacob and looked down at Faye.

"Who is he?" the woman inquired, her shrewd, brown eyes flicking toward the male rounding the cart.

"Your new teacher, Jacob Sorensen." He cleared his throat and offered a bow of the head in a show of respect.

"Ah, right! Well, do come in. I just put tea on, and the girls are currently studying, so it will be nice and quiet. I'll have a look at —what did you say her name was?"

"It's Faye, miss," Faye offered, her voice thick with exhaustion. Leon allowed for her to remain propped against him for support. Gods, he was warm and sturdy.

"Faye, what a lovely name. I'm Ms. Carmine, everyone here addresses me as Mistress. If you aim to stay here, that is what you will address me as, too." The words came out firmly, and somehow her tone remained kind.

"Yes, Mistress," Faye replied, her eyes wide behind the mask.

"Bring her inside, Leon, to the guest room. I have some things I need to discuss with Mr. Sorensen." She waved Jacob forward and into the home.

Inside the house smelled of spices which added to the warmth of it. A fire must have been blazing in a hearth because there was the fragrance of burning wood in the air.

Leon brought Faye into the guest room and sat her down on the bed gingerly. She felt the pillows, the raised fabric of the quilt, and although this situation wasn't ideal, it had little to do with Leon. "Thank you," she murmured and swung her legs up, whining as she did so.

"Don't move too much." His boots scuffed the floor as he moved forward, poised to help.

As much as her back protested when she leaned forward, she wanted to examine her ankle to the best of her ability. She let her fingers roam over the skin and cringed as she felt the protruding flesh, it was hot and puffy. If there were a break, she'd be in more pain...at least she thought so. More than likely, it was severely sprained and bruised.

"I'm fine, but thank you." She lifted her hand and patted at the air until she found his hand. Warm, strong and although she didn't know him, she thought it to be comforting, too. A smile touched her full lips as she squeezed his hand.

"You're very kind, Leon."

He inhaled a breath and let out a small laugh. "You get some rest. The Mistress will be in shortly." He turned on his heel and closed the door behind him softly.

W hen the adrenaline ran its course, Faye was weary down to the bone, her eyelids were heavy, and her body sunk deep into the bed. The lack of sight would be a challenge to grow used to, for it would always look like a moonless night to her.

She gnashed her teeth, cursing her sister, and she knew she had to be careful—Melothra wasn't a safe place for Faye, but at least she was nearly on the border of Alindor. Whatever Nymiane was planning, Faye had to return to Alindor as soon as possible.

Getting there was going to prove more troublesome than she anticipated. If she could steal a horse in the middle of the night and run, things would be easier. Yet how was she going to navigate the trails without the ability to see?

As Faye settled into a fitful slumber, her limbs twitched violently.

"Silly girl, look what you have done," a voice purred and was soon coupled with a laugh.

Blackness met her, more blackness, and when she took a step, she pitched forward. Her hands went to grab at the platform she had been on, but as she caught it, she found herself propped against the floor again.

A rush of air blew past Faye's face, and phantom fingers curled into her hair, causing pain to burst along her scalp.

"You're a lost soul just like the rest of them. Too bad you can't do a thing about this predicament."

Chilled lips brushed against Faye's hairline and elicited a gasp from her. Immediately, gooseflesh broke out all over her body, and she woke with a start. A scream was on her lips, but fear didn't grip onto her; no, she was furious.

Faye jolted upright, nearly colliding into another's head, and she would have if it hadn't been for the slender hands that steadied her by the shoulders.

"You're all right, Faye, you're all right. It's just me, Ms. Carmine." She shushed her, and as if handling a wounded creature, she began to stroke her back.

A frustrated sob left her. Why, why had she been sentenced here?

"I brought you a change of clothes, and since everyone is now calmer, I want to examine you. Come now, love," she said softly and aided in moving her forward. A breath escaped her as she took in the marks all over her body.

"Leon said you had run in front of his horse and that a wolf was nipping on your heels." It was a statement, not a question, but she wanted to prompt the girl into speaking.

"Yes, that's right. I… I woke up with a name on my tongue, but no memories." A lie, she hated the sound of it as it slipped from her tongue, but the truth would only sound bizarre at this point.

Ms. Carmine pursed her lips, her sharp gaze flicking over the bruised and battered form. "You are well-spoken, perhaps you're from a noble family. The name Faye is quite a bold name—being as how it is the name of the Lady of Light. " She eyed the quality of the dress, although it was currently as worthless as a rag, there once had been quality to it. Fine fibers and nicely stitched, it only seemed to confirm she was either a noble or a wealthy landowner.

"Some rest and food will allow your mind to heal, but for now, we have to get these filthy rags off of you. Are those cinders on your face?" She reached out to swipe at the smudge along her defined jaw. "Strange," she muttered.

It wasn't, not when the last memories were of a blazing fire, shrieks and the thud of her head against marble flooring.

Faye lifted her arms as Carmine prompted her to do so. She was vulnerable, but there was no choice in the matter. A more thorough inspection took place before she was bathed and fussed over. By the time it was over, Faye's skin was blushed.

Once she was seated on the bed again, there was a featherlight touch to her swollen ankle, the fingers were warm, and they seemed to spread a new heat through it. There were two kinds of heat: the dangerous kind where an injury radiated it, and then there was the good, the healing kind. This was the latter, and she felt the swelling recede, felt as her body began to relax because it didn't feel worn down.

Faye gasped, and she clutched a hand to her chest. "You have…magic," she whispered it, surprised.

A warm smile came to Ms. Carmine's features as she tugged Faye's skirt into place. "Our little secret. Some know, others don't. It is best it remains quiet, not all take kindly to people like me."

"Thank you for helping me, Mistress." She wished she could see her face, but the picture she gathered was one of warmth.

"Come, let's go meet the girls."

There was a moment of panic as she reached up to her face instinctively. "I don't think that is a good idea." She paused and then spoke again. "Mistress, what is this place?"

"A private school for the overprivileged." She laughed and shook her head, rocking back on her heels. "My darling, all the young women here are of noble blood. They come far and wide to study here. That young man, Jacob? He's a prestigious scholar that has come to teach the girls."

Oh, that was not at all what she had thought this was. She blushed furiously and chastised herself for thinking otherwise. There was a darker thought in her mind regarding what this place was.

Ms. Carmine tutted and gingerly wrapped her hand around Faye's bicep to guide her upward. Once she was standing on her slippered feet, she looped her arm through hers. "Anyway, hogwash that you shouldn't meet them. That is a bunch of rubbish. The girls receive oddities well. They are fascinated by them."

A huff of air escaped Faye, and she bowed her head as if to hide her face. "I don't like that I'm an oddity."

"Tut, love, aren't we all? You'll discover that, soon enough."

Outside of the room, Faye had no option but to rely on Ms.

Carmine to lead, and she clung to her like a lifeline. The house was less quiet than it had been upon entry and this time she heard the distinct sound of chattering females.

"Girls," Ms. Carmine began. "I'd like for you to welcome Faye into our crowd. She will be staying indefinitely." She pulled her arm away as she stepped aside.

They hadn't discussed how long she would be staying, but she felt as though that was her way of welcoming her for as long as it was needed. Beneath the mask, her cheeks flushed, and although she couldn't see the others, she could feel their eyes on her slender figure. They were assessing her, and Faye could not for a moment blame them.

"It's nice to meet you all." She waited for a hint of their aura, for anything to pop up, but nothing did.

"Some would call it blasphemous—being named after a goddess."

"I wonder if the goddess kissed her at birth!" a voice cried out.

"Why does she have a mask?" a voice whispered.

"Maybe she's disfigured," came a reply.

"Maybe she's ugly."

If only she knew the reason behind why it was on her face; she knew it wasn't because she had a scar or a deformity. The question was indeed why it had been placed there, to what end would this game bring them? She clenched her jaw, feeling hot tears burn her eyes which made her skin grow blotchy the more upset she became.

"Girls!" Ms. Carmine warned them, and for the moment they quieted.

"I think it is none of your business." It wasn't Ms. Carmine that spoke, it was someone off to Faye's side, and her voice possessed a thick accent. "If kindness were wealth, you two would be paupers."

"Zola! I appreciate the first sentiment but not the latter." Ms. Carmine lowered her voice.

"Yes, Mistress, of course." Zola fought back laughter, and it was discernable as her voice quivered, which made the others scoff in disgust.

"It's fine," Faye finally spoke, her shoulders somewhat squaring as she lifted her head. "I don't know why I have a mask on. I don't remember anything. I just woke up in the woods, and I had to run for my life." Lie, on top of lie. Although she didn't know why the mask was on her face, she did know who put her there and how she came to be there.

"Why?" The way it was asked implied disbelief. None of them except for Ms. Carmine, Leon and Jacob had seen the state she had been in when she arrived.

She could have decided to strike up an attitude, but she didn't. Instead, she replied calmly. "I was being attacked by a wolf. He had my dress and was chasing me."

"How in Etain's name did you run blinded?" It was a rhetorical question. "You are lucky you didn't snap your neck!" one of the girls cried out.

"I had no choice. I ran with my hands in front of me…" A lot of good it did her as she tumbled down the hill. Luck was on her side, though, as she had slid in front of the carriage belonging to Leon.

"Huh, well. I'm Shenae. I'm sorry I called you ugly." There was silence for a tick and then, "I don't think you'd be ugly. I mean, you have the most delicate chin I've ever seen."

A laugh escaped from Faye, and she surprised herself. "Um, thank you."

"How old are you?" another girl asked.

"I… I don't know. I can't remember." A lie coated her tongue, and she loathed it, it felt wrong to lie to them, but the truth would serve to complicate things, and no doubt bring trouble to them.

In comparison to those who came before Faye, she was young, younger than Nymiane and Etain, but still old as far as the girls in the house went. As much as she wanted to relinquish the truth she could not, not yet.

A white-hot pain flared in her head. She gasped and began to sink to her knees. She heard a hiss echo in her mind, felt vicious claws rake down her consciousness, and if chattering women had not surrounded Faye, she would have found it easy to slip away.

Slender arms slid around her waist before she hit the floor and Faye heard a groan in her ear.

"Elbow to the temple…ow." It was Zola. She had caught her.

"Bony little thing." She laughed and rocked back once they were both steady again.

"I'm sorry! Thank you." Awkwardly, Faye tried to compose herself, feeling far dizzier than she had before.

"Are you okay?"

"I keep getting headaches. They're enough to make me ill. I'm sorry I hit your head."

Keen brown eyes focused on the pair. "Well, now that is settled. Each of you come to greet Faye, close enough so she can hear your voice." Ms. Carmine instructed and motioned for them to move into a line.

There were so many names and different voices Faye knew she'd have a difficult time remembering and deciphering who was who, she sighed softly.

In total, eighteen young women were present, all of which were in the process of finishing up their studies.

"And who knows, maybe some of us will be chosen to attend Melothra's annual ball." A girl giggled as she tended to her needlework.

Zola smiled and tilted her dark head back. Thick dark curls tumbled backward as she eyed the other. "You wish to go then? I think it's overrated."

"What is Melothra's annual ball?" Faye inquired, reaching out with a hand to steady herself against the wall before she patted around to find a chair.

The room burst with excitement as the girls began to war over who would speak first. Somewhere amidst the chaos, Ms. Carmine had escaped the room and was not present to calm the girls.

"It's only the most extravagant event in all of Eudena!" cried one of the girls.

"Everyone hopes for an invitation, and it's a great honor." Zola moved closer to Faye as she spoke and patted her hand.

"Rumor has it that King Zev is in search of a wife, and this year's annual ball is meant to find him his other half." Zola continued, lacking the enthusiasm the others seemed to possess.

"Why do you not want to go then? If you had the chance at being the king's interest?" Faye did not understand, wasn't that every little girl's dream? At that moment, she wished more than anything that she could see the look on Zola's face, and perhaps she would have seen something that went unspoken.

"She's an odd duck, that's why!" one of the girls shouted with a giggle.

"Maybe I am, but I'm not ashamed of it."

And that, Faye thought, was precisely why she needed to befriend Zola.

After the excitement of supper died down a relative silence filled the house, the girls grew quieter, and the house's energy level seemed to drop. If it weren't for the clanging of dishes or the distinct sound of a broom scraping along the wooden floor, it would have been entirely silent. Only a giggle or a loud whisper broke what could have been complete silence.

Faye found herself shifting, everyone was applying themselves to a task and yet here she was useless. A frown tugged at her lips, and she sighed.

"Zola?" she called out, knowing from the sound of the smoky voice that she was nearby.

"Hm, yes, Faye?" She moved around a chair and stepped closer to her.

There was a pause, and then she spoke. "What can I do?"

Zola hummed as her slippered feet shuffled across the floor, her soft hands gently grabbing hold of Faye's bare arm. "We can talk. Everything is done, and we'll soon be in bed. Come with me." Tugging her arm, she led her outside onto the porch.

"You remember nothing of your life before the woods?" she inquired and cocked her head to the side.

The question Zola asked was complicated, and she felt compelled to tell the truth, yet this wasn't the time, not yet. "I wish I did. It would make things easier." Faye's full lips pressed together as she focused on the sounds around them. An owl hooted in a nearby tree and somewhere not too far off, a shrieking rabbit. It was a terrible noise, blood-curdling and yet it was the way of life.

An unladylike grunt came from Zola as she leaned close enough so that her breath mingled with Faye's. "Yes, it would."

She let her finger slide along the seam of the mask, and she tugged at it curiously. "Is it stuck?"

Instead of waiting for a reply, Zola tried to pull at the mask again, only when Faye cried out and grabbed hold of her hands did she cease. It was stuck.

"Unfortunately," Faye said miserably, as she cradled her face.

A wince scrunched Zola's features as she pulled her hands back. "I'm sorry!" she rushed out, biting her bottom lip. "We can work with it. Don't worry, we will figure out how to get it off."

"We?" She laughed humorlessly and changed the topic. "Zola, will you tell me where you're from?"

Guiding Faye toward a chair, she sat her down before she took a seat as well, arranging the skirt of her dress, she looked off into the velveteen sky. "That's a difficult story to tell. I'm from Nedrand, but my father is from Melothra. I've been in this house since I was twelve." She paused and let out a shaky breath. "He didn't want me—" The door slamming interrupted both of them; it was one of the other girls.

The melancholy in Zola's voice was nearly tangible, and there was more to the story, of that, Faye was sure, and yet she didn't want to pry. She had no business in that. Instead, she moved forward and grasped the other girl's hand.

"I have a feeling that we will get along well," she offered.

Once they were entirely alone again, Zola continued. "I didn't fit into his lifestyle, and I cannot say I blame him. My mother fancied herself in love with him, but to him, she was only a warm body. She passed away when I was twelve, and my father was contacted." Zola's eyes grew distant as she stared off into the woods. "I met him once, that was the day he picked me up and brought me here. Once was enough, I don't ever wish to see him again."

Faye leaned back against her chair and inhaled a deep breath of the damp night air. She felt it brush along her skin and absorbed the moment.

"I think we'll get along too, Faye." Zola relinquished her grip and let out an audible sigh, her arms lifted above her head before they came to rest behind her.

"I hope your memories return to you, too. A lot of hopes and wishes tonight. Hey! A shooting star!" She leaned forward and patted on Faye's knee quickly. "Make a wish!"

Zola shot up out of her chair and leaned over the porch's railing, her smoky green eyes following the trail.

Wishes only went so far, but dreams and aspirations were never-ending. Faye wanted more than anything to restore her prior life. However, there was a piece of her that was grateful for being here in this moment, learning about Zola, meeting Jacob.

A shaky breath escaped her as she began to stand unsteadily. "I think it's time for me to head to bed." She felt drained, and more than that, she felt oddly hollow like a piece of her was missing.

"Let me help you to bed," Zola said as she turned to face Faye. Without waiting for her to ask for help, she wrapped her arm through hers and began to lead her back inside.

Most of the girls were already inside their rooms, and the only noise in the main room happened to be a cat lapping at its paw. The occasional sound of embers shifting in the hearth coupled with the cat's grooming.

She lifted her hand out in front of her and tapped her foot, Zola had stopped beside her and cocked her head to the side.

"There's a wall here, isn't there?" She stomped her foot, not loud enough to disturb the house, but loud enough so that the sound bounced back to her. She couldn't go around stomping everywhere.

Zola pulled her arm away from her, and she watched with curiosity. "Yes, there is a wall there, be careful." Instead of rushing forward to aid her, she waited and arched a brow.

"Like a bat," Faye murmured with a hint of a laugh. She let her fingers caress the wall and began to slide around the wall into her room.

"Like a bat," echoed Zola.

"Good night, Faye."

"Good night, Zola, and thank you."

While this was challenging, it wasn't impossible, it was, however, going to take practice. Considering Faye had no idea how long she would be staying or where she would go, time was on her side.

No matter what, she would learn to see in other ways.

Once she climbed into bed, she began to wonder if she'd fall asleep at all.

The sound of the rain pelting against the window sounded painfully loud—it was funny how sounds seemed magnified when one's world was of darkness.

Instead of tossing and turning, she mulled over the facts of her situation. Nymaine, her sister, had thrust her from their realm in the heavens. But why? The question plagued her, and not only did she kick her from their world, but Etain had joined in the efforts, had successfully stripped her abilities from her and cursed her.

Jealousy was, of course, the first thing that came to mind, but it was more than that, and it was that thought which made fear and dread creep into Faye's bones. Nymiane wanted more than just praise and worship. She wanted everything.

When that wasn't enough to tire her mind out, she began to count the splatters of rain against the window. Somewhere around one hundred forty-five, she fell into a deep sleep, the heavy down blanket pressing against her slender figure.

At first, there were no dreams, no flickers of images, no sound, it was merely blackness, but then came a laugh; a laugh that was so deep and smoky that it made Faye's skin prickle in fear.

"Interesting, you don't know," the voice taunted before it materialized into a dusk-skinned woman. Her blue-black hair tumbled down, nearly brushing her bottom.

"What do you want?" Faye squinted her eyes as she peered at the approaching woman.

Faye felt as though ice ran through her veins and she had to bite her cheek to keep from speaking. The other's sharp blue eyes nearly shone against her darker skin which lent her a severe look.

The woman stretched her hand out to create an orb in the center of her palm, she cocked her head to the side and blew a breath at it. The sphere filled with smoke and when the smoke cleared, it revealed the shriveled-up figure of Faye in the woods.

"I am everything, and you are nothing. I have always wanted to say that." She laughed loudly and spun the bubble away, her fingers scrunching up the fabric of her black dress so she could stalk around Faye.

"I want to wake up now," she demanded.

"And do what? What can you possibly accomplish while awake?" the woman snapped, her eyes grew wide, and her lips pulled back into a sneer.

She looked at Faye as if she were a piece of dirt, and while it should have crushed her—should have made her cave—it inspired anger.

She lifted her hands to her face and felt there was no mask; of course, there wasn't, this was the dream world. It wasn't real.

"You will live a mundane life and die a mundane death. Sad, lonely and tragic," she began as she circled Faye. Nymiane's face contorted, reflecting how close she was to snapping altogether as if she were on the verge of plucking the proverbial wings from Faye. Contempt rolled off of her in waves.

Unwilling to merely listen to Nymiane's hatred spill forth, Faye turned away and balled her hands into fists.

"I wasn't finished!" she spat out and snatched up Faye's wrist. "Let it be known that you will die before the year is out, Faye. I will see to it. And you will never return to your seat in the heavens." Her lips cocked into a wicked grin, and she tapped at Faye's cheekbone, the tip of her nail grazing along the edge where the porcelain sat in reality. "Enjoy my gift," she purred, released her wrist and walked away.

Fear spread through her like a cold serpent, winding inside, tightening and threatening to suffocate her. She wished to crumple up on the blackened floor and yet she was furious, too. She jerked her head away at the touch and stared at the fleeting figure.

"Wait!" she cried out, taking a step forward. "Why did you do this? We are sisters..." she murmured and reached her hands up to her face where the mask would have been.

"Enjoy the rest of your dreams." Nymiane laughed until she faded against the black edges of the dream, her voice echoing.

A frustrated wail left Faye as she ran over to where the apparition had been, she struck the wall, and soon the floor opened up. She tumbled down into blackness until she felt as if a rope suspended her.

Her fingers wavered in the passing breeze, and when she brought her hand into view, the very edges of her hand had a faint glow to them. She flexed her fingers, stared down in curiosity and then swept her hand across the sky.

Stars shifted, realigned, and when she flicked her finger, one shot across the sky. Ah! She missed this. She missed being amid her realm and creating love, happiness, and beauty.

She scooped water into her hand, allowed it to trickle downward which created a rainstorm beneath. Each action was drawn out, and it felt like days had passed as she walked through this particular dream. When her eyes fluttered open, and she met the dreaded blackness of the mask; it had only been a night.

A knock sounded on the door just as she swung her feet out of bed, no stockings on her feet she shivered as bare skin met the cold wood.

Her body pulsed for a moment, she grimaced as a nauseating feeling swept through her. Something was off.

In a blink, the room illuminated and then faded to blackness once more.

"Just a minute!" she cried out and felt blindly at the nightstand. Panic lanced through her, she looked around and waited for the pulse to happen again.

It did.

The room seemed to shudder, color burst and faded into nothing.

"Come in," she muttered groggily. Her hair fell forward, shielding her face as she bowed her head.

"Sleep well?" the familiar voice asked.

There was no smile, and she was amidst trying to fight back vomiting. No part of Faye wanted Zola to see her in that state, she sighed and steeled herself.

"Well enough," she offered.

"Good enough!" Zola chirped and shut the door. "Mistress Carmine sent me with a new dress. Also, she wants me to help you."

She shuffled across the floor, laid out the dress and picked up the brush beside Faye's bedside. When she stood next to her, she began to comb out any snarls that had grown overnight.

"Thank you." She sighed. There was no way to thank her enough for the kindness she was showing.

"What? What is it?" Zola looked over to the dress as she combed out the tangled hair.

Amongst the house, she was already a novelty, a sort of sideshow attraction, but even in less than a day, Zola had managed to make her feel as though Faye had known her for a lifetime.

She felt comfortable.

"I had a weird dream, and I also keep having a surge of sight behind the mask." It sounded bizarre when she said it out loud, and it made her laugh.

There was silence and then Zola, not missing a beat, answered only, "Your dress, it's a blue one. Simple, but stately, since we don't need anything that fancy right now. Although, it does have embroidered flowers on the front." Her hand lowered so that she could squeeze her shoulder.

"It could be a potato sack, Zola, and I wouldn't know the difference." She laughed which was cut short as she moved too sharply and a piece of hair was yanked out.

"Goddess, I hope you'd notice the difference in quality." She snorted.

"Good morning, girls!" Ms. Carmine crooned. "Breakfast is ready, situate yourselves, don't dally because Mr. Sorensen will be handling your classes today." She nodded and flicked her wizened eyes toward the approaching young man.

"I hope you're all ready to begin your studies. It is my honor to teach you." Jacob surveyed his pupils and offered a slight bow of his head.

Faye smiled as she listened to him, gathering up her skirt so she could begin walking toward the table. Whatever happened in the dream world allowed Faye to actually see in a different way. She might not have seen definition, but she saw whirls of color, auras and felt intentions. She was able to see enough to move safely and not need to rely on someone to help her.

"Enjoy your breakfast, and I'll see you all shortly." Jacob smiled and offered a bow of his head before departing the room.

Zola stood next to her and as Jacob left the room, she let out a laugh. "Sorry, I have a story to tell you," she murmured.

"Oh?" Faye blinked, her head moving to follow the retreating figure.

A laugh escaped her again as she nodded. "Oh, yeah, let's eat before we're pulled away to study."

They moved to the table and took up seats next to one another. Curiosity struck Faye, and she found herself yearning to know what was so funny. She shifted her jaw as she took up a napkin and placed it on her lap. She fumbled a moment as she searched for her utensil and when she found it, a sigh escaped her.

Around them, chatter filled the air as all the girls began to whisper and the dining area was soon full of life, laughter, and companionship.

"So, before Mr. Sorensen, we had another scholar come to teach us. He was with us for several years, but our Mistress discovered he and a girl had taken up a relationship with one another. When the relationship became more involved, and she couldn't hide it for long, if you know what I mean—he was promptly fired after the discovery. The girl begged to be released with him, and it wasn't up to Mistress, but rather the girl's family." Zola shrugged and began to peel an orange before placing a slice of it in her mouth.

Faye's mouth gaped open, whatever she had been anticipating, it wasn't this. She moved her head, drinking in the figures that sat around the table, wondering if that girl was still here.

"She's not here," Zola began, "she was released per the request of her family. Last I heard, she married the scholar and they have three children now. The Mistress has been in charge of our schooling for a while now, she hasn't exactly trusted anyone else to take over, but she must trust him." She nodded toward the doorway in which he had left.

"He's a good man, Zola," Faye offered, not that she knew him for long, but she knew enough, she saw more than another person. Anyone could lie about who they were and what type of person they were, but no one could disguise their aura.

From what Faye saw, Jacob was almost as pure as they came, as flustered as he might have sounded with Leon, as well as grumpy. He was genuinely kind.

"We will see," Zola offered, disbelief shadowing her features, but she said no more during breakfast and instead packed food away.

Taking the hint, Faye followed suit and decided to listen to the conversations around her to see if she was able to learn more about each of the girls.

They did not disappoint.

The girls filed from the room once breakfast was complete, they began to migrate down the hall, and Faye followed. Two doors down, there was a large room. There were several pine tables with benches to sit on. Each table became occupied with several of the girls, and their books, as well as parchment paper, were laid out before them.

She could have snorted at the situation. Instead, she sighed and turned to her left, Zola wasn't nearby, and when she searched the room for the familiar whirl of colors, Faye did not find her.

Zola had filed out at the same time as everyone else, but she was missing from the room. Curious, she thought and huffed to herself.

"Something wrong, Faye?" a voice asked, sounding genuinely concerned.

She found herself the center of Jacob's attention, which swiftly turned to the entirety of the room. Quickly, she decided that to make it believable, she had to look discomfited.

"I… it's personal," she whispered, hoping that he believed that she was in need of using the privy.

He flushed and nodded his head. "Oh, of course, you're excused."

She thanked the old father Akos that came before her and stood from her seat, carefully maneuvering her way out of the room. Winding her way down the hallway, she allowed her hand to run along the wooden walls, and she listened carefully to the surrounding sounds. She heard a voice, loud and commanding, —Ms. Carmine.

"Now, now, focus. Peer deep inside of yourself," she chided the other. "Good, just like that, now what do you see?"

There was a pause for a moment.

"Light and blood. Alindor's king—and, oh! Goddess, Faye!" It was Zola's voice that rang out in panic.

Startled, Faye gripped the wall and leaned in closer. She clenched her teeth together to keep from gasping and tried to still herself. Carmine held magic in her veins, and Zola it seemed, too, and a seer to boot. What had she seen, though? What of Alindor's king, blood, and light. She tried to piece these things together. It was arduous with a seer's abilities. Some things were literal, and others were signs that could have been anything.

"What of the king, Zola?" Carmine prompted, trying her best to keep her voice steady.

"I don't know, it happened so quickly, I don't know, but Faye, *Faye*, Mistress!" she gasped out and stood up and quickly fled the room.

"Zola!" she cried out and briskly walked to the door, only to let her go.

Prying herself from the wall, Faye began to walk down the hall as if she were venturing to the privy, she heard Zola's footsteps stall behind her and half expected her to call out, yet no word came. A frown marred the lower half of her face as she heard the footsteps lead to the stairs, and like that, Zola disappeared to her room, leaving Faye to a silent misery.

Rather than hunt her down, she left her alone and opted to return to the classroom, just in time to be greeted with what benefits the teachings held for the girls.

"Inevitably, you will all be wives one day, some of you will be wives to nobles, others will not be so fortunate, but one thing will set you apart from the general mass of women, which is your mind. One must never underestimate a mind, it is our most powerful tool, and with it anything is possible." Jacob looked around the room, lifting his brows at the handful of girls that scoffed at him.

"As if anyone would believe us wise and intellectual."

"If you don't believe in yourself, why on earth would a potential suitor, who likely was taught not to consider your mind? I speak from experience, ladies. When you open your mouth, do not prove them right, prove them wrong in a tender way."

"A tender way?" scoffed another girl.

That was enough, these girls did not see the point, and Faye was growing tired of the small-minded behavior. "What he means is, you don't have to be cruel with your intelligence. Belittling someone who doesn't know something isn't kind nor is it necessary."

"Exactly, thank you, Faye." He nodded his head in appreciation and began the rest of the day's lesson, and for the remainder, the girls listened to him, and in turn, he allowed them to voice their opinions, to talk and learn.

He was indeed a good man. Words aside, she was able to see through him, to what mattered most and he shone radiantly. Jacob would be a grand addition to the program if what he opened with was any insight into his beliefs.

Although her thoughts kept drifting to upstairs, she endured the teachings of Jacob for the remainder of the class.

"How mundane," drawled Nymiane.

As the words met her ears, Faye felt herself being submerged into darkness, like someone was pulling her into the deepest part of the water where no light entered. She gasped and choked, clawing at her neck.

"Father didn't teach you enough? Do you have to sit through mundane teachings? Pathetic."

Faye's body shook, which made her brows lift, she peered down at her hands and felt her shoulders tremble. Asleep, she thought, she had fallen asleep.

She opened her mouth to fire a retort. She choked on the words as she endeavored to shout in the thick darkness, but in one sharp jerk, Faye awakened.

"Faye!" the female's voice cried out.

"I fell asleep," she murmured, brushing her hair back she began to stand.

"Sit, don't move," Zola ordered and sat on the bench beside her. "Don't. Move." Huffing, she swept back her hair and eyed Faye. "Are you okay? No one is here but us, everyone left. Mr. Sorensen didn't want to wake you."

There was a long answer, and then there was a shorter

answer. Shrugging, she turned away from Zola. "I'm okay. It was just a dream."

"The kind of dream where you gain partial sight even though you're wearing a mask?" She sounded perturbed.

It didn't make sense why she'd be infuriated with her, unless she was still upset about the vision earlier, in which case, she wouldn't blame her. "I think maybe I should go outside and catch some air."

A sharp intake of breath was followed by a curse, one that gnawed at her because perhaps Zola deserved to know the truth, but what would come of it? Would it merely put her new-found friend in danger? She wanted to apologize for withholding the truth, but wouldn't the apology just be digging a hole and incriminating her?

No, for now, the two of them would keep their secrets from one another, and Faye knew that she would wallow in guilt because she knew what Zola's secret was.

She didn't excuse herself or say a word as she stood from the bench and left her alone, it would seem the two of them both needed some time.

The fresh air tickled at her nose, the scent of the decomposing leaves made the air sweeter, especially since it had rained overnight. There was a certain peace to be found amidst the woodlands that were good for a being's soul, a place where one could absorb the forces around them and be still, to merely ground themselves at that moment.

Faye stepped from the porch and onto the grass, feeling the slipperiness of the leaves beneath her shoe. She bent down, picked them up and allowed her fingers to run along them. Cold to the touch and they were not yet crunchy, and they still had some life in them.

Off to the side, the sound of a man's chortle sounded, curiosity getting the better of her, Faye followed the sound. Outlines of the barn came into her vision, and she managed to see enough so that her gaitm while careful, was still even.

Hens clucked as they pecked away at the ground. A gander alerted them of Faye's arrival, spreading his wings and declaring her an intruder. It made her laugh, but to his credit, he didn't so much as nip at her skirts.

"Someone is coming," the male said quietly.

Flushing, Faye realized maybe she shouldn't intrude, but it was a little too late as Ms. Carmine erupted from the barn. Her hands were tidying up her white hair.

"What the good goddess' name are you doing out here, girl?" she asked softly, but there was still an edge to her tone.

"I needed some air, and I heard a noise," she pointed out, having the decency to look away.

The man lumbered out of the barn, clearing his throat. "Sorry," he mumbled in a familiar bashful way.

Leon. Leon and Ms. Carmine? Faye twisted her lips to keep from smiling, but it didn't work so well.

"Oh! Leon," Ms. Carmine waved at him, casting her eyes over his taller figure. Evident affection glimmered in her wizened gaze, but neither one said anything or reached for one another now that they were ousted.

"I promise not to say a thing. It isn't my business." Faye lifted a finger to her lips and began to turn on her heel.

"No, you stay put, Leon has to get back to work," Ms. Carmine paused to eye Leon and jerked her head. "You and I need to chat about something."

With care, they both walked into the barn, the sweet musk of the livestock permeated the air, and the abrupt warm, whiskered nose against Faye's chin made her jump. A warm breath flooded her neck, and she laughed. She lifted her fingers and felt along the contours of the creature's face. A horse.

"That is Sarge. He's a good boy. He is the color of steel, unique, even as he's aged he hasn't lightened a smidge. Some believe that Etain touched him in the mare's womb. A gift from the goddess!" Ms. Carmine offered and watched Faye closely.

The name Etain almost made her flinch, and her fingers stopped along the velveteen ears. Etain did not like to meddle with mundane affairs, and she left most of them up to their free will. To take time out of her day to touch a horse seemed unlikely, but who was Faye to thwart that notion?

"Isn't that a lovely prospect," she forced herself to say and avoided looking at the mistress altogether.

"Faye, would you tell me if you had any abilities? I don't mind harboring those with talent, but I like to know what I'm dealing with," she inquired.

That was more than fair, she nodded her head and let out a heavy sigh. "Not quite abilities, but I can see somewhat, by way of outlines... I can peer into a person's aura and feel their intentions."

A *hmph* came from Ms. Carmine as she rapped her fingers against the wooden stall door. "And these are not considered abilities?"

When compared to the flood of strength and power that she possessed, this was nothing, this was not even child's play in the heavens. This was a teardrop-size of power when Faye could create an entirely new skyline with a stroke of her hand, craft a sunset with just a thought; this was a tease, which was why Nymiane granted it to her.

"I suppose they are," she offered softly.

"Be careful, Faye," she whispered as she reached forward to grab one of her hands. "Be careful, if my gut tells me true, and if... the forces agree, be careful." She bowed her head and kissed her knuckles softly.

People like Ms. Carmine, Zola, Jacob and Leon, they were in danger if Nymiane gained control of Alindor, and there was the sneaking suspicion she had her sights on Melothra, too.

Three weeks passed by like a breeze, and the house settled into its routine once more. In spite of the recent changes, everyone fell into step, Faye had become one of the girls, and it was as if she had always been a part of them.

There was one thing that struck her as odd, however. In the past two weeks Zola seemed to distance herself from Faye, and had they not been nearly glued to one another's side the first week, she would have thought nothing of it.

"We have the luxury of an adventure today," chimed Clara, her voice breaking into a fit of giggles.

"An adventure?" Faye questioned.

Zola sidled up to her and patted her arm as she let out a throaty laugh, her green eyes sparkling with mischief. "Yes, we are allowed to go into Kyrrjath. There is a small festival, and it's fun. All of the local girls run rampant through the streets and select their ribbons, mask and gather ideas for their gowns. It's all in preparation for the annual masquerade."

"They can't keep us inside of Piram forever, the countryside is lovely and all, but *goddess*! How are we supposed to learn to be ladies when we're closed off to society?" Clara's tone took on a dismal quality. She made a face, and in spite of the look, she flounced off to nag one of the other girls.

Zola's sudden appearance startled Faye, but it was more the physical touch which had been absent for at least a week. Come to think of it—she had made herself scarce with just about everyone lately.

"Good morning, ladies," a male voice sounded.

"Good morning Mr. Sorensen," all of the girls chimed.

He cleared his throat and assessed them. "I'll be riding with you into town. I lost a few supplies on my trek here. Ms. Carmine will also be accompanying us."

Faye shifted, although the prospect of venturing out was indeed exciting, she also felt a ball of nerves form in her stomach. She could have sworn she heard a faint laugh in the back of her head but shook it off.

"You will be fine, we'll be together, and we have to find your accessories," Zola began to list off what they needed and shook her head.

Did she believe that Faye would venture to the masquerade or that she would ever receive an invite? She was an unknown with no title here, and no claim to great lineage.

It must have been written across her face because Zola chirped, "Where there is a will there's a way."

"Alright, girls, eat your breakfast and then we will be off into the city," Ms. Carmine said in passing, but she didn't remain in the room for long. She motioned for Jacob to follow suit.

At the table, Faye maneuvered around with more confidence, her fingers found purchase on a spoon, and she began to eat. She hadn't realized just how hungry she had been, and rather than speak, she busied herself with the food.

Once finished, each of the girls filed out of the dining area and fetched their reticule before bounding outside. Faye had nothing to her name, even the dresses she had were borrowed, but she went along happily. However, she needn't worry for long because Zola soon looped a spare reticule around her wrist and led her outside.

"I don't need anything, but you... you could benefit from owning something that truly belongs to you."

"But does it? I appreciate this Zola, but I cannot take your money," she murmured as she touched the velvet bag.

"I don't need it," Zola insisted, her voice gaining a small edge to it that brooked no room for an argument

As much as she may have wanted to argue, she was beginning to realize that Zola became rooted in her opinions and seldom budged. With a nod of appreciation, Faye disputed no more and let it be.

Outdoors, she smelled the browned leaves of winter, the musty scent coupled with the crisp air tickled at her nose. She smelled the sweet, earthy scent of the horses, too. She heard the sound of their breathing, felt the ground tremble a touch when one stomped at a pesky black fly. A smile tugged at Faye's lips as she reached up to touch one of the horse's muzzle. Soft, prickly, warm and wet.

The sound of the girls clamoring into the carriages and chittering away made her smile, and soon she was climbing into one as well.

Today would be an adventure, Clara had spoken true. As foreign as everything felt to her, Faye was genuinely looking forward to mingling out in a city.

Some yearned for a fantastical adventure off slaying dragons, but for the moment, going out into a busy city was Faye's fantastical beast. Perhaps she could recover some memories while she was there.

The horses launched off into a steady trot, and instead of watching the blurred lines flicker by, she closed her eyes and absorbed the other facets that surrounded her—the smells, the taste, the feel and she found herself laughing.

The sounds shifted from the lively forest to that of a thriving city. Horses' hooves clattered on the streets; vendors barked out prices and items as they attempted to gather interest in their wares. The smell of spices and smoke filled the air, but it was the presence of a significant number of people that made Faye's heart pound.

"And, as if you couldn't tell, we are here!" Zola announced as she looked around happily. "Are you okay?" she whispered close to her ear.

Having to think for a moment, she pressed her lips together. "Yes, are you?" If she were honest, she felt strange, mostly because as of late Zola's behavior was, well it was downright alarming.

Jacob walked up to the side of the carriage and extended his hands to the girls. "Watch your step," he reminded them as he took their hands and helped them down.

Faye offered him a smile, grateful that her hair tumbled into her face.

"You look radiant," he remarked as he tilted his head to take in what he could of her face.

The bruising had long since faded thanks to Ms. Carmine's talents, her hair was brushed, and she wasn't curling in on herself. She did look much better.

"Thank you. I feel much better."

His hands went up so he could help Zola down, too. "Enjoy your day out, ladies." He chuckled.

The wind picked up, which lent the air even more of a bite than it had previously. Faye was suddenly grateful that a cloak had been offered to her, which she tugged around herself tighter.

"There is a stall with hot cider up ahead, and it'll warm our bones and belly while we browse." Zola tugged on Faye's elbow, although at this point it wasn't entirely necessary.

Faye's footing had become more confident, and while she had a companion to guide her, if she found herself floundering, she could ultimately feel her way and vaguely even see.

Reaching out, she took up a cup of the cider, offered coin, and began to sip at the contents. In its wake, it left a warm path which sank deep into her bones.

The hood to the cloak offered a buffer between her skin and the biting wind; it also shielded her from curious eyes.

Down the crowded roadway, they came to a halt—she looked back and forth trying to find the edges to the establishment they were in front of but could not distinguish them.

"It's a mask shop," Zola offered and guided Faye inside.

Inside, it smelled musty, like old boxes and books with a hint of polish. Mannequins wearing elaborate masks decorated the walls; some had fascinators attached to them while others were simple in design.

If Faye could have seen it, she would be surprised, but judging by the deep intake of breath beside her it must have been marvelous.

The shuffling of feet brought Faye's attention toward the left side of the room. She could determine where the individual was and offered a nod of the head.

"Good afternoon, my ladies, what can I help you with?" the portly man asked.

"We are looking for something extravagant, something that

would steal the breath of one of the goddesses, something that would make even the goddess Nymiane green with envy." Zola laughed.

However, there was something about the name Nymiane that felt like a knife twisting in her mind, she winced and let her shoulder lean against Zola.

Faye's mask could not and would not be able to come off. From what she heard it was simplistic, no definition, no curve around her lips, just a pure white slate of porcelain that stuck to her face.

The vendor's frame shifted, and he stroked along the underside of his chin. "That is a bold request," he said and turned toward the many masks he had on display.

Zola moved forward with Faye in tow and swept her gaze along the shelving. One of the mannequin heads wore a beautiful mask that made her gasp.

"This one, I like this one," Zola said. "Are these real diamonds?" They beaded along the brow, just tiny ones, but it made it glimmer in the sunlight.

The vendor snorted and puffed his chest out. "Of course, I don't make my living ripping people off, besides… that's where the money is." He winked.

"Ah, Faye," Zola turned toward her and began to describe it. "It's the loveliest shade of blue, with black accents and the diamonds pop against the dark colors. It would look lovely with your complexion."

Faye smiled, it was kind of her to include her in the shopping spree, but honestly, there was no point in it. Besides, if it had diamonds, she wouldn't be able to afford it even with the pouch that Zola offered her.

"You should get it then," Faye suggested.

"It wouldn't work with my complexion. I need green," Zola began to say and was cut off by the vendor.

"I have green!" He lifted a finger and spun his large frame away so he could produce the mask. "Here." He handed it over and brought forth a mirror so she could look at it against her skin.

The dusky quality to Zola's skin was paired nicely with the vibrant, dark green.

"I'll take both." Exchanging the money for the masks, Zola

steered Faye away and continued toward the alluring scent.

"What is that smell?" Faye's mouth watered in anticipation, her stomach rumbling. Breakfast had only been two hours ago, but that sweet, spicy smell was enticing.

"That would be the most delicious thing you have ever tasted in your life." She laughed and pulled her along.

A sticky bun from the mortal realm, Faye mused, would it compare to the foods she was accustomed to eating in her domain? She didn't know, and she didn't care, neither did her stomach.

Happily, she followed Zola until the scent was so intense that Faye began to lick her lips. She lowered her hand to her belly and felt it growl against her palm.

The fragrance grew more potent, spicy, sweet and now distinctly buttery. "Jhra's sticky buns, they're rolled in local spices, and he sprinkles nuts on top. The honey that is drizzled on top brings the flavors out," Zola explained and plucked two up.

Faye bit into it, and if she thought it had smelled lovely, then this was heavenly. The honey complimented the flavors, and she savored it. "Jhra is talented and should never cease to make these," she began to say as she when she pulled away from the stall. "But what if I want more?" It was a large pastry, so one should have been enough, still!

They both laughed as they milled through the shops, savoring their treat. "I think you should opt for a dress that would match your mask. That same brilliant blue, and crystals that look like diamonds."

She might have meant well, but Zola had to know that Faye would not receive an invitation, she was a nobody, and what was more than that she could never afford a dress as elegant as the mask.

Pressing her lips together, Faye opted to let Zola run away with her fantasies, it wasn't as if she would be able to tear her from the topic, that much she knew.

"Oh," Zola gasped and halted in her steps.

Faye turned her head to regard her. "Are you okay?"

She made a noise in the back of her throat and stepped backward, guiding her to a wall. "I'll be right back, okay?" Zola slid away and left her alone.

S tanding by herself, she felt how vulnerable she was, her heart sped up, and she listened to the sounds of the people, the rustling fabrics, and chatter as they milled by. Zola's behavior lately was more than peculiar. Faye's hand splayed against the nearby building, and as the moments ticked by rather than feeling panicked, she began to relax.

The feeling soon faded, her body lurched backward as strong hands pushed her into an alley. She felt as though she were falling and would have if it hadn't been for the hands securing her in place.

A scream almost escaped her, but a voice was soon shushing pleading with her to remain quiet. It made Faye want to panic all the more.

"Please, please don't scream. I promise I'm not going to hurt you, I promise, I do. Just don't scream." His voice was soft, imploring even. His grip loosened on her, green eyes focusing on her masked face.

As Faye's vision blinked, she could see the soft outlines of his body, and a subtle glow surrounded the male figure. She wished she could see him, but this would be good enough.

"What are you doing?" Faye asked firmly, not trusting him. They weren't that deep in the alley, she hadn't stumbled back far enough, and if she chose to raise her voice to alarm someone, they would have heard her.

A growl sounded in the street— something that sounded like "where is he?" or "where did he go off to?" But the male that the voice belonged to grew distant.

"Did you steal something?" she asked.

"Oh, heavens no!" He laughed, deep and genuine. "I wouldn't

steal—" His words halted as he pulled a hood up to cover his features.

"Are you okay?" he questioned, lowering his voice as he moved in closer.

She swallowed, what could she come up with that didn't sound silly? "Startled, but I'm okay."

His gaze swept along the masked features beneath the velvet hood, but he said nothing, and instead, moved to rest his back against the wall. His breathing eventually settled into a normal rhythm.

Faye swallowed and wondered when a comment would come, but it never did. He never mentioned her face, never asked why.

"You smell like sticky buns," he said with a laugh.

Perhaps she should have been embarrassed or taken aback at the less than smooth remark, but the truth was Faye found nothing in it but humor.

A surprised laugh escaped her, and she covered her mouth, half wondering if it brought attention to them.

He shushed her with a laugh.

"I just ate one."

A disgusted sound escaped him and a rustling of fabric as he shifted his legs. "I haven't had one in what feels like forever." His hand reached toward hers as he looked down the alley. "Be careful. There is garbage all around." As if to prove his point he toed a glass bottle away from her feet.

This one certainly had an odd way about him, she thought. "What is your name?" she asked boldly.

There was a pause, too long for it to be normal.

"Sandor," he whispered and waited for a name in reply.

"Sandor," she echoed and then replied with her own in return, "Faye." If that were his real name, she would have been surprised, given that pause before he answered. She quirked a brow, but it went unseen. "You don't sound like a Sandor," she teased.

He snorted. "Oh, I am, I definitely am." Sandor didn't sound too pleased about that fact.

"Do you often hide in alleyways?"

"Only when I'm craving sticky buns," he supplied, chuckling more to himself than anything.

The colors around Sandor shifted, they held light tones that contrasted with the distinct blackness that surrounded him. It pulsed blue, yellow and gold, which gave her pause. She had once seen one with colors like these, long ago and those memories made her mind ache.

"I won't tell anyone where you're hiding."

"Much appreciated, it would cause a great disturbance in the marketplace," he muttered his words.

If Faye hadn't been close by him, she would have missed what he said. "So, you're on the run? Are you a prisoner?" she inquired.

He sighed heavily, leaning his head against the brick wall behind him. "Unfortunately... I am running, but I didn't steal anything, and I am most certainly not a prisoner..." His breath blew through his nose, and he sounded quite indignant.

Whatever question had been on the tip of Faye's tongue had fled because she heard a growl escape someone. This time it wasn't a wolf from the woods, this time it was distinctly human.

A sneer warped the face of a guard. "There you are." His voice lowered.

As she turned her head toward the direction the voice came, she made out the colors surrounding the individual. They were not unlike those that surrounded Sandor, whatever that meant.

No curse left Sandor, but another breath did, and it sounded like relief.

"Sandor...?" Faye called out and blindly fumbled toward his direction.

"Don't, there's a whole bunch of junk back here, but I've been found out. My time is up," he murmured.

"Oh, your time is definitely up." The guard's eye sparked as he shook his head and advanced toward him, a metal plate covering one eye glinted in the sun.

There was no way out of the alley, if by chance Sandor could scale the brick wall, then perhaps he could leap from rooftop to rooftop, but he didn't seem inclined to do so.

Faye was in no position to argue with a guard. In her passing through the streets she had seen dark shades, red, too, and felt her skin prickle as she walked by.

Sandor strode forward, hands extended as he offered his

wrists to be shackled by the guard. His hood shielded his face from the view of the public eye.

Iron manacles clicked into place, and though he couldn't see beneath Faye's hood, he offered her a wink in passing. "I have no doubt we'll see each other again," he purred.

A startled laugh escaped her. "How?"

"We are both suckers for those sticky-buns."

"Faye?!" Zola cried out urgently, zipping by the alleyway. "Oh, goddess, Faye where are you?" She spun around in place, frantically looking. Panic etched itself in her features and crept into her voice.

Sandor lifted his shackled hands and kept his head bowed, and he thumbed in the direction where Faye was and walked ahead of the guard.

Zola gave him and the guard a questioning glance but followed his direction as she stumbled into the darkened alley.

"I'm here, I'm right here," she called out.

"Oh, goddess, don't do that to me again. I thought I had lost you and it would have been my fault, please don't do that," she prattled on and gripped her head in panic. "I won't leave you again, just promise to stay with me?" she asked.

This was not at all like her, and it was concerning. "Are you okay, I didn't mean to worry you," she offered softly and took her hand to squeeze it.

She said nothing in return and instead began to lead them out of the alley.

Faye's gaze drifted toward where Sandor had last been, and as they passed a guard, a blur of colors rushed upward from where Sandor was walking, he clucked his tongue and let out a songbird's note in the form of a whistle, letting her know he had seen her.

She smiled and continued the rest of the excursion with Zola.

Zola eyed Faye dubiously. "Why were you in the alley?"

The hood to the cloak began to fall, and Faye snatched it up quickly, tugging it into place. "Why did you run off?"

A snort escaped her friend's mouth. "Touche, anyway, the seamstress shop is up here."

Even if curiosity gnawed at Faye, she didn't expect Zola to divulge anything, not when she was unwilling to do the same. If it were important, Zola would have told her.

Venturing inside of the shop, she was met with a distinct smell, old wood, and dusty shelves, it smelled much like the windows were never opened, but amidst that was a floral note. A tickling, confusing scent when coupled with the overall fragrance of the room.

"This woman knows her designs, she's a little kooky, but she can whip up a beautiful gown that is out of this realm."

Wandering around the shop, a middle-aged woman soon approached the two of them. Her hair was curly and white which contrasted with her dark skin. Alarmingly, her eyes were so light green that it gave her an otherworldly appearance.

Something dropped in the room, and it made both of the girls leap and turn around.

"Zola!" she exclaimed and rushed up to embrace her. "Eeeeka, look at you, you grow more beautiful by the day." She turned her attention toward the cloaked figure of Faye, arched an eyebrow and let one of her hips drop.

"Breshia!" Zola rocked from side to side and then squeaked when the woman tweaked her nose.

"Who is this?" She made a noise and began to walk around Faye, her hands brazenly grazing along her curves, tugging her arms out of the long sleeves of the cloak and even pushing back the hood.

Faye gasped, she began to step back and shy away from the woman's invasive touch, but she merely continued to tug, pull and shift fabric.

"Pah! I've seen worse, trust me... I've seen worse," she reiterated what she had said by lowering her voice. "She's petite, that hair... in my youth, I had hair as black as this." Breshia wound a finger around her hair and took a glimpse at it, her eyes narrowing on the traitorous white strands.

The woman had seen worse, and the word made Faye grimace.

"I'm not going to ask the story, we all have one, and some are sob stories, some are gleeful, but wherever you came from doesn't matter, girl. Where you're going matters, what you do now matters, yeah?"

It didn't matter— as far as Faye was concerned, her slate was blank and all she had was the present, which had been eventful. From the moment she had awakened in the forest to now, so much had occurred, and it felt strange to her.

Breshia swept her hand in the air and narrowed her brows. "Come, come, let me see the masks then, I know you have them," she demanded.

Zola pulled them out with care and laid them on a nearby stool.

"Oh, this one," she said as she picked up the blue and black one that was for Faye. "This one is for you, isn't it?"

How she knew was anyone's guess. "The blue one?"

"Mhmm, that one, the hair, skin..." Breshia paused and pushed back the fabric of the cloak to inspect Faye's neck. "Beautiful neck and collarbone. Hmm, yes."

"I assume you want to keep the masks until you've selected the fabrics, per usual?" Zola asked.

"As always, my dear, as always. Have you any ideas what you'd like for style? Or the usual?"

"Usual, but I have an idea for Faye's." A mischievous look washed over her face as she stepped up to Breshia and led her back to the counter, whispering low enough so Faye couldn't hear.

"Oh...that is lovely, yes... I'll have to get my sketchbook out and draft that immediately. You'll trust my ideas?"

"Always, Breshia, always! It's why I keep coming back here."

"How are things?" Breshia inquired, there was something in the way she said it that made it clear she wasn't talking about life in general, but a specific matter.

"Good, things are good."

Faye began to turn to leave them to their chatter, but a hand came to rest on her upper arm, stopping her from moving away.

"Take caution, My Lady, Three moons in the sky, one amiss, another defied. The last and third of most import could very well disrupt the court," Breshia spoke in riddles. She blinked and pulled back her hand as if the contact burned. She swallowed roughly, hands folding in front of her. "Sorry about that," she murmured.

She looked alarmed, sheepish even, and her tone was meek. A stark difference from moments ago.

Within, Faye felt something stir, she acknowledged the words but what they meant was unknown to her. Breshia hadn't called her girl, and it had been My Lady, which was what patrons called her.

A hand came to her throat, between this and Zola's vision nothing good was ahead of her, perhaps this evening she'd ask Ms. Carmine what her translations were. It was just too strange and coincidental to hear two predictions.

It was time to go.

"Send word once you've finished, Breshia. I can't wait to see what you have in store for us," Zola said, smoothing over the awkward tension that now rippled through the room.

"She's a Seer?" Faye asked gently, not wanting to spook Zola. No one else in the carriage could hear above the squeaking wheels and the clip-clop of the hooves.

Panic filled Zola's eyes as she bowed her head and hissed, "Don't say that! Someone will hear." No one was in danger of hearing unless someone counted the wind.

A moment went by, and she was so quiet that Faye didn't think she would bother to answer, but then she curled an arm around her shoulder and began to talk.

"She is, but she hides it well. Melothra isn't keen on those with supernatural tendencies. Breshia says that it's a gift from the Northern goddess, both beauty, and talent." A small laugh escaped her, and she sighed as she continued. "But she usually has a firm grasp on it. She tries not to touch people, and she sees things most that way. Sometimes her ability is so strong that she doesn't need to come in contact with someone.

"If anyone were to find out, Breshia could be used in so many terrible ways. It's best if it remains a secret."

"Of course, I would never say a thing." And she honestly wouldn't, as if she knew much of anyone to blab to, but more than that, it was Breshia's secret to hold. Whatever was wrong in Melothra had little to do with Faye, even if she longed to fix it, the fate of the country was out of her hands.

The knot that formed in her gut began to twist and pull, causing her mouth to pinch. A headache formed along her brow bones and she wished to the heavens above she could remove the blasted mask, to let her skin breathe, to feel the sun on her flesh and to be able to see a person as she spoke to them.

Each of them grew quiet, and the rest of the voyage back to Piram was filled with companionable silence.

Evening painted the brilliant sky hues of orange, red and pink, causing the trees to look as if they were on fire. An ornery rooster crowed into the fading light, disgruntled with the mere fact he couldn't fight the loss of daylight.

The excursion had taken the entire day, and Faye was exhausted, the constant wandering around took its toll on her back as well as legs. In short, she ached and throbbed all over. What was more than that, Zola had walked away with the others into the house and left her alone.

She didn't dwell on that thought for long, because the shift of shadows brought her attention to the only figure in the room.

Jacob tugged his cloak off, shaking it out before he hung it up on the rack. His attention turned to Faye, and he hurried up to her.

"Here, let me help you," he offered and pulled the cloak off. Turning, he hung it up on the rack and studied her. "Are you okay?"

There were many things she could reply with, that she was okay and that it was a thrilling day, but she opted for the honest answer. "I'm very sore and exhausted. I'm also confused." She promised she wouldn't say anything about Breshia, but it didn't mean that she couldn't talk about it.

"Want to talk about it?" he inquired.

"Maybe tomorrow," she began.

"The others are going to bed if that is what you're concerned about," Jacob said, testing the waters.

Faye did want to talk about it, and she was more than willing to, but Zola had rushed off to her room without so much as a good night.

His head popped up, and he motioned for one of the kitchen staff to fetch some tea and something to eat. "Did you have a good time in Kyrrjath?" He led her to a chair and once she sat, he followed suit.

A smile tickled the corner of her mouth. She did enjoy it. There were some delightful moments, some heart racing, pleasant ones. "I did." She paused, her fingers tugging on the sleeve of her dress.

Jacob waited, his body pushing back into his chair. "And yet?"

Faye lowered her voice, she wasn't sure if anyone was listening, but she would make it that much more difficult to eavesdrop. "Someone came up to me, mentioned three moons, each one had a part to play. She told me to take care." Goosebumps lined her skin, and she shivered, in spite of being sat in front of the roaring hearth.

He listened carefully, his eyes sliding to the leaping flames as she finished. "Our goddesses, they're often referred to as the moons. Each one does have a part to play. What else did she say?"

"One was amiss, one defied, and another had something to do with a court," she fumbled over her words trying to recall them.

"Some say the goddess of the North has turned her eye from her people, and that she has allowed for her Southern sister to rule supreme. I don't believe it."

"You said there were three," she said.

"Mhmm, Goddess of the Middle. Some say that she has aided her Southern sister in removing the Goddess of light."

Faye's heart hammered in her chest, her stomach nearly dropped, feeling betrayal stab at her heart once more. Nymiane and Etain might have been step-sisters, but they were still sisters to her. It was no secret they harbored hatred for Faye and yet she had always loved them. They would sneer and laugh at her goodness, at being the goddess of light. She clenched her hands in her lap as she considered these words. "Maybe they are the moons."

Clattering dishes on a tray made her leap, she sucked in a breath and shifted in her seat. "Sorry," she murmured.

"No, it's okay. Are you all right? It's a possibility, although, if that is true, then you spoke to a Seer; they're not common these days. Be sure to keep that to yourself."

"I will," she paused and then, "Jacob, where are you from?" The idea of her sisters plotting her death broke her heart, but more than that, it filled her with renewed fury. She would not make it so easy.

He laughed, pouring them both some tea and handing her a plate of fresh bread, with melted butter. "Alindor. The kingdom of light and beauty."

"What is it like?" she asked, wanting to hear it from a mundane's perspective. She took up a piece of the bread to nibble on.

He hummed as he sipped his tea. "Oh, it is quite possibly the most beautiful place," he said carefully, minding his choice of words. "The North Sea glitters like diamonds, the sunset is positively breathtaking, and the people are genuinely kind."

Faye saw it in her mind's eye. A bleached stone palace facing the open water, with windows taller than a man to allow sunlight to pour in. The streets were bustling with life as they gave thanks to their patron goddess of the light. Gifts dotted along each of the citizen's doorsteps as they exchanged gratitude with one another.

Lost in these images, she felt the teacup slip from her hand, and the last thing she recalled was the panic in Jacob's voice, trying to call her back, trying to wake her.

"*Just what do you think you're doing!*" a woman's hissing voice called out. Shadows flocked to the figure, clinging to her like sordid pets.

Faye blinked her hazel eyes, trying to focus on the slithering apparitions before her. "You! What do you want! Is my mortality not enough for you?"

Amusement flickered across the other woman's face, but a sneer distorted it. "*Oh, little Faye decided to grow a backbone, did she?*" she cooed as she stalked forward, bent down and cupped Faye's chin with cold fingers. "*I'm tired of how you are playing a weak fool; that is not why you are there. We have bigger games to play, little one.*"

She jerked her chin away and swiped at the hand which held her in place. Narrowing her eyes, she rose to her knees. "I am not playing any games, Nymiane," her voice sounded foreign to her, more commanding.

"*I sent you to create something, not hide in some musty house playing damsel.*"

"Create what?" she shouted, dark hair tumbling over her shoulders.

Nymiane's features smoothed, she waved her pets away to reveal her beautiful face. In her hands she held a mirror, she spun it around, so the glass reflected her face.

"*Now, that is for me to know and for you to find out, soon.*" She laughed and dipped her head forward, baring her teeth in a cruel smile. "*But take a good, long, hard look at this face. The beauty your people revere...*"

The mirror showed her face, but mortality didn't mar it, it was smooth as porcelain and without blemish. Her hair was as rich as it once was, but it was her eyes that held something else —something new—and it terrified her. "No," she whispered.

"You had so much spark before, why extinguish it now? I sincerely thought you'd fight more than this. I didn't take you for a weakling," she crooned.

A noise escaped Faye, and deep burning anger ignited in her belly and before she knew what she was doing she lashed out, her hand connecting with the dusky features of Nymiane.

She stumbled back, snickering as she lifted a hand to wipe along her cheek, crimson flecked her fingers. *"I always knew how to get under your skin, Sister."*

Although Faye had slapped her, she felt just as stunned as though Nymiane had done it to her. "You dare call me your sister after all of this?"

"You're utterly useless like this, and I'll do us both a favor and pull some strings." She stalked forward, and as Faye began to evade her, she commanded the shadows around them to bind her. *"You're in Etain's country, and you'll find your powers weaker here. And this?"* She used a nail to motion toward the shadows. *"The shadows are stronger here than in Alindor, you're halfway to my realm, Sister, and you're going to suffer."*

Suffer, as if she hadn't suffered so far.

A wry smile curled dark red lips up as if she had read Faye's thoughts. *"Oh no, you haven't suffered. Do you think wearing a mask is suffering? Do you think being housed with people who support you is suffering? You have no idea what true suffering is, Faye; none. I will gladly show you, and I will revel in watching you fall to your knees begging me to stop it."*

White, blinding light exploded from Faye. She lobbed a handful of it not at Nymiane but the darkness she brought with her.

"You have no idea!" Nymiane laughed, her black nails scraping along her cheeks as she stared at her. *"None! You were always his favorite, his beloved, and how the people favor you. No more, the mortals will pay for their loyalty."* A wicked gleam entered her glowing gaze. *"And if they choose to worship you still, they will crumble alongside your temple."*

Shaking, Faye squared her shoulders. "You will not!" she cried out.

Nymiane's hands were on her, though more akin to talons,

and they were beginning to bite into Faye's shoulders. Lines of red dribbled down her skin and stained her dress. *"Don't doubt me, little sister, but here is a gift to you."* With brute force, Nymian shoved Faye's slender shoulder down and pinned her with a forearm. With her free hand, she slammed her palm against Faye's forehead.

Memories flooded into her, of a blazing fire in her temple, discarded oil lamps littered the floor and trails of oil ignited. Etain had assisted Nymiane, had bound her, cursed her, and sent her to the mortal realm. Tendrils of shadows encased Faye's wrists and gagged her mouth, stripped her of her immortality and threw her into the realm of humans.

"No! You won't!" Faye thrashed to the side, dislodging her sister, and crawled after Nymiane's discarded form.

She only laughed, her hard, blue eyes gleaming. "It has already begun. You may want to wake up—Jory? Oh, what was his name?" She clanked her nails together, propping herself up on her side.

A snarl ripped from Faye, launching at Nymiane she grabbed her by the shoulders. "You will leave Jacob alone, and you will leave all of them alone." She lifted a hand and smacked her, letting her nails cut a trail along her dark cheek.

As much as she wanted to do more, she felt her knees weaken, and the grip on her sister loosened.

"I told you, you hold little power here. You'll grow weaker, too, as your people begin to realize their Lady has turned a blind eye to their pleas."

The curse was the most infuriating thing. Nymiane had ensured only one could take it off, and that one would be driven to madness, and chaos would erupt.

"You feel it, don't you? Your power is drifting away." A mockery of a pout curled Nymiane's lips as she gave her sister's cheek a gentle pat. *"It's time to wake up now, Faye, at least now you know. It's time to make yourself useful."*

Faye's fingertips clawed at the stone ground, her chest heaving with the effort to grasp something, anything. The last thing she wanted was to be pulled back to the mortal realm, mainly since she was face-to-face with her wicked sister.

"You will not prevail, Alindor will still thrive and no matter your plan—" she choked on her words and finished crumbling to the ground, unconscious.

Nymiane lifted a brow. *"Sorry, I didn't catch that,"* she crooned and faded into the darkness.

With a start, Faye came to, her eyes opened to meet familiar darkness and a string of curses left her. She turned to her side to seek Jacob out but found that she was no longer in the comfort of the house, instead, of a swaying carriage. To further confirm that, the sound of the horse's hooves deafened her. Frustrated, she cursed again. Whatever Nymiane was planning was sure to be dreadful.

"Let me go at once," she commanded, hands bound at the wrists with strong rope. She thought of Sandor in the market briefly, and his wrists bound in manacles.

A grunt came from the nearest guard, and he had the good grace to sound apologetic. "We cannot, I'm sorry."

"Of course, you can," she replied tersely.

"Wh-what he means it that, should we disobey orders, bodily harm will come to us or those we love."

"Immediately," the other chimed in.

Silence passed between them, and Faye shifted her jaw. "Where is it we are going?"

"Dyphren. The palace, to be more specific."

What awaited in Dyphren? The capital city held no import to her, and all that came to mind was the temple. It belonged to Etain. She was less vile than Nymiane, or at least she had thought so. This move against her painted her in a different light.

"And?"

"We don't know anything else," his voice softened.

A moment ticked by and Faye turned toward the closest guard. "What happened to him, the man I was with?"

"He's all right, we dosed his drink just as yours was, he's likely awake now, right as rain." He seemed to read the look on her face because he nodded as if to say he was telling the truth.

A hiss came from her as she bowed her head, fingers meeting

the smooth plate against her forehead. Of all the schemes Nymiane ever had, this one took the cake.

She had always been wicked and jealous regarding how the people adored Faye, yet seemed to curse Nymiane. Could anyone blame them? Her land was full of turmoil, civil wars were always on the brink of erupting, and they loathed their goddess.

Instead of growing weakened by this, she drew power from their chaos, their hatred, and illnesses.

"I swear it. He is going to be okay." He grimaced and settled into his seat, keeping his eyes lowered.

"I believe you," she offered and turned her head to gaze upon his figure. The imagery intensified. They were no longer blurred lines, there were almost complete figures, and it was wholly their essence.

In spite of the deed they had performed, there was no indication otherwise in their auras that they meant harm. "What is it she is holding over you?" Faye asked softly.

A sour look passed over the older guard's face. "My wife and children," he offered.

The other remained silent for a moment before speaking. "My sick twin sister."

Tensing, Faye leaned forward. "Then bring me to Dyphren. I will figure this out." She clenched her teeth together, seething, and folded her arms across her chest. The rocking of the carriage served as an agitation rather than something soothing as it had been not long ago.

Sleep longed to take Faye, but she refused to give in, it was where her sister took pleasure in torturing her, and she would not give her the satisfaction of another round of it.

The carriage tilted around a corner, causing her to reach out and steady herself. Outside of the window, she could see the patrons of the city milling around. Behind them loomed shadowed buildings, merely an interruption against the colorful array of auras.

Much to Faye's surprise, a crowd already gathered, and it made her wonder if her arrival was anticipated. They drove through the city, it wasn't as bright as Alindor, although it was to be expected. Even with her full vision, Melothra as a whole was darker, somber in color.

As they halted in front of the palace, the clanking of armor sounded, and the door to the carriage opened. Faye was ushered out and felt much like a spectacle. All around them, people stared, her hood had long since fallen to her shoulders. Wild, dark hair framed her masked face.

They walked along the courtyard until they met the dark stone steps. The guards that flanked her grabbed her elbows to aid her up the first one, even though she didn't need it, she did nothing to dissuade them from helping her.

Even the palace was dark stone, not bleached like that of Alindor and not black like that of Nedrand.

Figures moved at the top of the steps, and they parted to allow a tall man through, his aura was nearly as dark as the stones they stood on. Judging by the crown that adorned his head, Faye gathered that this was the King of Melothra.

Chapter 9

"**W**hat have you brought me?" His dark green eyes roved over the bounty in the guard's grip.

They exchanged looks with one another, deciding whether or not to divulge the truth in front of an entire crowd.

"A woman of talents," one of the guards offered quietly.

"I'm not in need of a concubine," he sneered and began to turn on his heel.

"Your Majesty!" The older guard winced as he raised his voice.

King Zev raised his brow, jaw clenching at the bold speech. His lips pulled back into another sneer as the guards nodded to Faye.

"We have a message, but… it is best to be done in private." He looked over to the growing audience.

The king appraised him, waved his hand and turned on his heel. "Impress me."

Faye tugged her arms away from the guards and mustered some dignity. It wasn't their fault, not when they were being held against their will, too.

They were led down a long corridor, the smell of spices hung heavily in the air and tickled her nose.

Eventually, they made it to a meeting room where the king sat at the head of the table. The guards didn't bother sitting, nor did Faye even attempt to.

"Begin," Zev prompted.

"Your Majesty, this is the goddess Faye, Lady of Alindor," he said, his voice quaking.

Faye gathered that if Nymiane had not threatened them

personally and clawed her way into their minds, that they wouldn't have believed it either, which made her wonder how they were supposed to convince King Zev that she genuinely was the Goddess of Light.

He shot a doubtful glance toward the bound figure and ran a finger over his lips before he let out a deep laugh. "You think me a fool?"

The men both stammered. "No, Your Majesty!"

Tilting her head upward, Faye settled on the dark figure in the chair. "What they say is true, and I can prove it." She shrugged away from the guards and began to walk toward the king.

His personal guards raised their weapons, ready to use them. "Let her come, she's bound, and a slip of a thing, I could knock her out." He laughed at the thought.

Nymiane must have had a reason and a plan behind placing her here, she'd trust her sister enough to send a message along.

In spite of the worry she felt building inside of her, she remained composed as she approached Zev from the side. "Take my hands, if you may," she said steadily, extending her bound hands.

When he did just that, Faye felt revulsion ripple through her, his hands were coarse, but more than that, she the felt wickedness pouring from him, which warred with her goodness. Of course, her sister would choose him of all people.

A grunt came from him, expecting some sort of show and when he was about to move away his body jolted.

King Zev cried out, his guards rallying to his side and on the brink of spearing Faye, but even if they wanted to, they would not, for dark ways were at work.

Shadows surrounded him, Nymiane's voice whispered and coaxed him, teased him even.

"Use her, she's a weapon. She is yours to use, yours to wield. Do not take her to Alindor, but bring Alindor to you. We will watch them fall and bow to us."

King Zev's pupils were blown wide as the shadows circled around his chair, tickled along his skin and crooned to him, seducing him, pleading with him to give in and use the weapon that held his hand.

"Take her bindings off," he said as he released a breath,

motioning toward his guards. "You've done well to impress me, you're excused." He jerked his head toward the door and focused the entirety of his attention on Faye.

"So, you really are the Lady of Light. How the mighty have fallen." A laugh escaped him as he stood from his chair, cupping her slender chin in his hand. "Alindor will fall, it's only a matter of time. And those people you so love will fall with them."

Faye knew of the discord between the two countries, knew that King Anmar had no love for King Zev and his ways of bowing to Queen Majidah's every whim. She didn't realize that Nymiane had poisoned this country as well and was on the verge of poisoning another.

Where was Etain?

Shifting her jaw, Faye regarded the king coolly. "My people are stronger than you think, and they are a good people—" she began to say.

" — and without their goddess influencing them, they will rot, too, and they will need someone to swoop in and save them. Their doe-eyed royals are too soft to oppose anyone."

That was the general consensus when it came to Alindor, they were too busy praising their Lady, celebrating love and peace ever to be considered a viable threat. However, she knew better and knew that Alindor kept it a secret, too.

"Besides, Anmar's beloved son and heir have turned up missing. I wouldn't be surprised if someone took him and planned to off him. I bet his pretty head would fetch a hefty sum."

A pit formed in her stomach as she searched her memories for the king's son. It was a well-known fact he kept his son hidden away—not locked in a tower, but out of the public eye. No one knew what he looked like. Prince Roshan was indeed their prized gem.

"Ah, so you believe it, too?" the king inquired, smirking.

"No, I believe them wise enough not to show their hand to enemies." Faye clasped her hands in front of her, squaring her shoulders.

She didn't realize what had happened until she found her palms resting on the cold floor. Zev had struck her face, which had been half protected by the mask. Her jaw throbbed, and if she could have mustered even a trace amount of her power, he would have felt her wrath.

"Bring her to a room. I have some things to think over." His eyes moved along her body, and he nodded.

These guards were not as kind as the ones who brought her in; they were rough and their grip unforgiving on her skin. She was furious, vulnerable, but above all else, she was useless which enraged her.

She could not protect her people.

Nymiane would win if she couldn't think of something. More specifically, Faye needed to be in Alindor. There was hope that being in her land would ease some of the restraints on her power.

As rough hands shoved her into the room and slammed the door shut, she heard the tell-tale click of a lock sliding into place. Escaping this place would not be easy, especially given her limited vision.

She turned on her heel and bumped into a pillar that held a vase on it. Faye let out a frustrated growl and swiped at the glass which sent it flying to the floor. Soon, she sunk down into a sit and bowed her head into her hands.

"I never did a thing to you, Sister, ever," she whispered.

"Father always favored you, doted on you," Nymiane replied, taking on a physical form in the room.

"All of this because you were jealous?"

"No, all of this because *I can*. Also, to showcase I am capable of more than what I was given."

"What have you done with Etain?"

"Etain is occupied, worry about yourself—or don't—it's not like I care. Enjoy the show." She snorted.

A moment later, Nymiane was gone. Faye needed to be alone to mull over what could be done. With her temple in ruins, it meant her people could not gather in droves, the truly faithful would continue their worship at home, but what would become of her when the masses ceased?

The brisk wind rustled the sheer drapes against the windows, it whistled softly and drew her toward them. Wincing, she heard the crunch of glass under her foot and was thankful she still had her shoes on.

As she moved forward, her fingers found a knob, and to her surprise, she discovered it was a door. She turned it once and found it opened. Perhaps they figured a blind woman wouldn't try to climb down a few stories, and they'd be correct in that assumption.

Air washed against her skin, and since the sun had long since settled down beyond the horizon, it had become chilly.

There was movement below, and she half wondered if she should step back, that if she didn't, then perhaps this little freedom would be taken from her, too. A moment passed and then another; maybe she was safe since no cursing or shouting came from below.

"It's supposed to freeze over tonight, shouldn't you be bundled up by a fire?" a voice called from below.

Startled, Faye gripped the railing to steady herself. "There is no fire in my hearth, and I'll be fine just the same."

"I can come up there and start one for you, if you'd like," the same person offered, his tones rougher.

It was tempting, but for one, a servant could do that, if they were even allowed to, and secondly, Faye simply wanted to curl under her blankets and sleep. Perhaps her dreams would offer some resolution to all of this.

"No, I'm going to bed, and it won't be needed. Thank you."

A pause from below and then, "Surely, you'd like the warmth of a blazing hearth. It's going to be unseasonably cold tonight," he murmured.

Faye's lips twitched in annoyance as she moved her head to peer down at the wavering figure. His aura was bright, with many colors, there wasn't an ounce of ill-will in him. He was being quite pushy, which made her wonder why.

"And why, pray tell, are you being so adamant about the hearth?"

"I didn't get that far in my plan," he admitted.

"You have a plan?" she asked, confused.

The sound of rustling plants brought her attention toward the side of the balcony. The guard was beginning to climb the thick ropes of a vine, only pausing to grab the railing of the balcony to hoist himself up onto the landing.

"Albeit a terrible one, but it is a plan," he laughed his words, slightly breathless.

Faye crept away from the balcony rail and toward the door.

The guard lifted a finger to his lips, likely out of habit—she couldn't see him as another could, but she saw his movements as wobbling images.

"You don't belong here, that much is clear. I don't mean to startle you, but I'm going to help you get out of here." He motioned toward her features, the pale quality of her skin. Amongst a sea of dusky tones, Faye might as well have a target painted on her back.

"Aside from that, I tried your door and found it locked. So, you're definitely not a guest of honor."

She shook her head and squinted her eyes, she could almost make out his features. There was a distinct shadow on his face, one that she couldn't see fully, but make out enough to know it wasn't. "Do you have... A mask on?" When the words escaped her mouth she regretted them, it was rude to ask, she supposed.

His lips twisted into a grim line. "I do. Scarred in the line of duty, I'm afraid." It was only a small piece that hid the corner of his eye, it was fitted against his brow bone and beneath his eye, so it covered just below his cheekbone. It was a dark metal plate, with silver scrawlings on it.

To his credit, he didn't point out the mask she wore or ask why she wore it. Instead, he turned on his heel and walked into her room. The hearth was cold and had been cleaned out, the guard didn't hesitate to toss in some logs. His hand found purchase on the ledge above it where he extracted a flint, his fingers pulled on the tuft of cloth around his neck so he could light it.

Worn fingers tore the fabric so the tiny fibers were exposed. He kneeled down before the hearth and removed his flint, gathered up some kindling and struck the flint until it produced a spark large enough to set the fabric on fire.

Soon, the fire blazed, the tell-tale crackling and the scent of smoke washed over Faye's senses.

"What is your name?" she inquired.

His feet scuffed on the floor when he moved away from the fire, and he exhaled a breath. "The less you know of me, the better, but know that I am a friend."

The clink of the flint on the mantle blended in with the

crackling fire. "I guess that will have to do for now," she offered softly.

"Have patience, My Lady." His voice held laughter as he approached her. "Your knight in shining armor is bound to arrive."

There was something familiar about the wry way he spoke, and she found comfort in that. "I'm afraid a knight will do me little good in this situation." That was putting it mildly, no mortal would be able to stand in the way of a goddess' wrath.

He scoffed at that. "Everyone needs a diversion."

"Is that what you are? A diversion?" She stepped away from him and toward a seat, lowering herself into it.

"I never once claimed to be a knight. I am a humble servant of the people," he offered in a playful tone.

"Of King Zev, you mean." The room was beginning to warm, which encouraged her to shed the cloak that was wrapped around her form.

"No, of the people. I serve the crown, but the one who wears it is ever changing. To serve the crown is to serve the people and country."

He spoke eloquently for a guard, perhaps he was a noble that was turned over to the crown, who could say? Faye's nose wrinkled as she regarded him.

"Wise words from a humble servant."

He bowed to her, grinning. "I try. As much as I'd enjoy pondering on life's idiosyncrasies, I have to return to my post. I'll check on you tomorrow."

"That won't be necessary," she began.

"Maybe not, but it won't stop me from doing it. Have a good night, Lady."

Instead of using the door, he opted to use the balcony again, scaling down the overgrown vines in that same way he had done on the way up.

That night, it was a dreamless sleep, much to her disappointment, nothing was revealed to her and Nymiane for once stayed away for the duration of her slumber.

Chapter 10

The next morning, King Zev pushed his way into Faye's quarters. "It's time to wake up, Lady." His dark eyes pinned her prone form, and he shook his head.

Faye jolted to consciousness and pulled at the blankets to shield her form. She wasn't naked and couldn't discern where the king's gaze was, but she felt like he was peeling away the layers.

"I'll have new clothing brought in for you, no need to embarrass yourself or me for that matter with the rags you're wearing."

They were not rags, it was a delicate dress, as elegant as any courtly lady's dress, but it was the wrong color for the king, that much she knew.

"Today, we have some important people to meet, so you will dress as any of my guests would." In accordance to what he deemed fit, of course.

"I am not a guest though, I am your prisoner. You will not succeed, I vow it."

A laugh escaped from him, his ring clad finger lifting to wag at her. "I think I like you. You have a fire in you. I've been waiting for a wife, maybe it's time to settle." His gaze roved over her slender figure.

Faye felt bile rise in her throat. Marriage amongst the heavens was not unheard of. A union had not been celebrated in centuries, not since her father married Isha, Nymiane and Etain's, mother.

"Am I not good enough for a goddess?" he sneered.

"You are not good at all," she spat out.

"It's a good thing I don't need to be." His lips spread into a vicious smile as he walked out of the room, slamming the door behind him.

Faye leaped from her bed and hissed in frustration. Her fingers dug into the fabric of her dress, scrunching it up in her grasp.

If Zev got his way, he would pry the mask from Faye's face somehow to unleash a new terror on the world, she knew it, and his intentions were clear. He wanted her for himself, which made her stomach roil again.

A knock on the door caused her to startle, and then a soft voice came from beyond.

"Hello? I'm Luta. I'm just here to prep you for the day, m'lady." The girl moved closer, tentatively until it was clear she was allowed to approach. Carefully, she began to undo Faye's dress before she slid the mahogany colored one over her form.

The fabric clung to Faye's form, two strings dangled in front of her. She felt at them, but the maid's deft fingers were quick to swipe them away so she could tie the halter portion of the dress back.

"You will want to gather the excess of the skirt in your hand, there isn't a lot, but there is enough so you might trip over it." She bunched up enough of the fabric and placed it in Faye's hand so she could gather an idea of how much to hold.

Guiding her to the vanity, the maid sat Faye down. "Your hair is lovely, it should be showcased." That was all she said before she began to work on it. When she was finished, it was only a simple coronet braid with the rest her hair down. Simplistic, yet it was wholly Faye.

"And you are ready for breakfast, His Majesty awaits you." She didn't wait but instead went ahead and escorted her to the dining hall.

In those moments, Faye attempted to count the steps, note the turns of the hall and commit every inch she could to her memory.

"Ah, so nice of you to join me, Faye." Zev purred his words, not bothering to stand from his seat at the head of the table.

He knew very well that she had no choice in the matter, and if she did, there was no way she would be dining with him. However, no food had been brought to her last night, and the last piece of food she had was the sticky buns in the market.

At the memory, her stomach rumbled in protest. She sat opposite of the king, which suited her just fine since she was a great length away from him.

The servants milled around, depositing food on the table. The scent of freshly cooked meats, bread, and some fruit tickled her nose.

"I like this color on you better," he mused out loud. "All that is missing happens to be a gold crown."

"No," Faye said firmly. "Nymiane may have stripped me of my birthright, but she will not win, and when this comes to an end, I will not forget what the King of Melothra has done."

Zev's face darkened, his lips pressing into a firm line. He was a handsome man, but his wickedness bled outward. Instead of smiles, he wore scowls and his dark eyes were filled with contempt, if he had an ounce of light in him, he honestly would have been enough to inspire dreams in the heart of every young woman.

"You are mortal, Faye, and as such, you will not prevail. Your patrons grow tired of your silence, their crops are failing, their prayers go unheard… Their faith is dying and it is poisoning Alindor. In less than a year they will turn to a new ruler—a new way of life—or die. "

With each word, Faye felt her gut twist, his words were like a knife driving deep inside of her. That was how deities died, they were forgotten, and the faith perished with them.

If it were possible to touch Alindor's land, if she could feel her home again, then there was hope that she could heal her people.

Soon, the chairs filled with bodies and Faye felt her skin crawl in their presence. She felt their wickedness oozing from them, and it made her ill.

"These are notable men and women of the kingdom, you will see them at the ball, Faye."

Clenching her jaw, she swept her gaze across the table, refusing to let a frown pull at her lips. In her lap she clutched her napkin, working her fingers against the rougher fabric.

"I suspect you have no need of the ball now since you've found your prized wife," one of the older gentlemen said.

"Perhaps. I won't be seeking a wife, but the masses would be put out if I canceled it, and to declare myself engaged would no doubt cause an uproar before the event." He ran a finger along his full lips.

"Thank you," Faye offered to one of the servants as they filled her goblet with wine. Greedily she drank it, wishing it would dull the rising dread. They all mulled over what the marriage meant, but Zev failed to mention who she was, and of course, they did not question their king.

"Why the mask?" one of the women asked, sniffing.

"It will be a grand unveiling to all that evening. the King of Alindor will be there, and I want him to see my bride." An unspoken hatred coated his words, and it caused the rest at the table to either murmur to their neighbor or remain silent. "I believe you will inspire a great many things, my beauty," he said, allowing his eyes to drink in her figure greedily.

It would surely inspire something.

Breakfast, for the most part, remained uneventful. Faye did not so much as look in the direction of the others, and it wasn't because she feared them. No, if she had any plan on retaining the food she ate, she could not.

Once the king relieved her from the room, she found herself face to face with the guard from last night. Cocking her head to the side, she took in his stance, friendly and open.

"I was told you were allowed a walk in the garden if it suits you," he offered.

Allowed, she thought miserably. "Thank you," she murmured as they began to walk outside. "Tell me something, is it true Alindor is crumbling?"

There was hesitation on his end, and he exhaled heavily. "Not entirely, but since the sudden destruction of their Lady's temple, it hasn't been the same. They quarrel, they suffer, and they're angry." He didn't speak from a place of prejudice, but rather sadness—that much was evident in his tone.

Was it safe to speak to him? Could she, in fact, trust him? "What of the king, is he preparing for an uprising...or worse?" she inquired, carefully stepping into the garden. The air was cold against her skin, but it was welcomed at this point, for it soothed her.

"I don't know much, My Lady, I know that he will be at the ball for a meeting with King Zev, that is all. I'm sorry."

"It's not your fault," she sighed her words. "Still, won't tell me your name?"

A grin crossed his face as he walked down a row of evergreens with her, his worn fingers skimming along. "I suppose since you're here for the long haul, it won't hurt, it's Jaran."

Committing the name to memory, Faye nodded her head.

"Have you decided what you'll be wearing to the ball?"

A scoff came from her, and she whirled on her heel to consider him. "That's a strange question coming from you, and no I haven't."

"Strange? I'm trying to make conversation, but if my opinion is anything, I'd say that a blue and silver mask would look stunning on you." He shrugged and began to walk away from her.

Faye reached out, snatched his wrist and pulled on it. "What did you just say?" she whispered, unsure if anyone was listening to them.

"I'm a friend of a friend, your knight is on the way," he offered slyly.

There was only one person who knew the color of the mask that had been chosen, and of course, the dress was designed after it. "My knight?" A puzzled expression crossed her face at the cryptic words, but she said no more and released his wrist.

His brows lifted as he laughed. "Yes, she's quite bold," he murmured, his eyes warmed.

Jaran had spoken to Zola, how he managed that, she didn't know, but it warmed her heart, especially to think of Zola as a knight in shining armor. "She will be here, for the ball," Faye said softly.

He hesitated, his lips pulling back into an uncomfortable smile. "Yeah, she will be." His hand scrubbed at the back of his neck, he was withholding something, but Faye was growing used to that, to not knowing everything.

"Okay, I can endure this, it's just a month's time before the ball, I can do this." She nodded her head and spun on her heel to finish her walk through the garden. Jaran followed her closely but said nothing.

A month dragged on, during which King Zev had forced
Faye to endure his companionship during dinners,
which meant she was carted around like a show pony.
He had, in fact, the good graces to allow her to select a seamstress of her choosing, and of course, she sought out Breshia.

When they were alone, Breshia had nearly broken down into
a fit of tears. Faye hushed her and assured her that all would be
well enough. Good could come of this still, she had promised
her.

The second meeting with Breshia was when she brought the
finished dress the night before the event and the mask that
matched it. Faye smiled down at the mask in her hands and
thought of the marketplace, of Zola and that strange meeting in
the alleyway.

"I shouldn't say anything, but I wanted you to know that the
Lady of Alindor's light has spread to parts of Melothra, not all
worship Etain here." Maybe Breshia simply wanted to comfort
Faye, and it did, but those of Alindor needed to worship her, too.
Idly, she wondered if Ms. Carmine had anything to do with this,
considering her denouncement of living in Melothra.

"Have they begun repairs at all in Kathill?" she asked softly.

"Yes, it didn't all collapse, the walls have been replaced and
the altar, too, but Faye has not returned to Alindor." Breshia
eyed her meaningfully.

"I need to get there, somehow." Desperation crept into her
voice, but the time was drawing near, her patience was running
thin, and her people could not continue to suffer. Without her
presence in the kingdom, she had no doubt that Nymiane would
make her move.

"Oh, My Lady, stay strong, this soon will come to an end."

Perhaps she knew what would transpire, who could say? In the end, all that Faye could do was play her part and do so wisely. "Thank you, Breshia, blessings upon you."

Tonight was the night, the King of Alindor would be present, Queen Majidah as well, and every one that was of importance— which meant the single noble ladies —would also be there.

Faye swept her hand down her gown, the beautiful mask was laid over the plain porcelain one, and rather than pin her hair back in a chignon for the event, she kept it down, with sparkling diamond brooches inlaid in her hair.

The banquet hall burst with life, the minstrels played loudly, and although she began the night by the king's side, it would seem he had other plans that involved the Queen of Nedrand. The announcement would come at midnight, which meant she was left to her own devices.

She frowned as it was announced that the King of Alindor would not be attending, that he had taken ill, and it worried her. Had Nymiane set another plan into motion?

Zola was bound to be here. With hope flaring in her chest, she began to maneuver her way through the crowd of individuals, her fingers scooping up the excess fabric of her skirt. A sour look came across her face as she stepped on something gooey, which distracted her for a moment. She caught herself just in time before she slammed into a solid figure. Their shoulders scarcely brushed.

"Apologies," the male offered, collecting something in his hand.

"It was my fault, I stepped in something…" She blinked, the scent of honey, nuts, and spices wafting around her.

"Probably a sticky bun, they are devilishly delicious— but they are a mess," he said with a laugh.

Something tickled at the back of her mind, the way he said sticky bun. "Is that what these are?" she asked excitedly and reached forward with a hand.

"Allow me." He put his plate aside and scooped up one for her, offering it to her. "Melothra knows how to perfect them."

Picking up his plate, he began to savor the pastry. "Goddess, I've been craving a sticky bun for weeks," he murmured with a laugh.

"Sandor?" she asked quietly, quiet enough so that it was only for his ears. She hoped it was him, but why would he be here? She pulled back her head and took in his garb as much as her vision would allow her to, and she found her mouth gaping open.

"Small wonders," he said softly, and then, "One of my many names, but few know that one." His pale green eyes slid to her face, and he finally took note of the porcelain behind the other mask. Recognition dawned on him, and he exhaled. "Faye, from the marketplace... Will you walk with me?"

He didn't have to ask her twice, Faye glanced over her shoulder to see if Zev's aura glared in her direction and when she saw no hint of him she allowed for Sandor to escort her outside on the terrace. "How are you here?" she asked, doubt creeping into her tone. "You were running from a guard."

A snort escaped from him. "Not true, I know the guard. I... well, I'm the Prince of Alindor, Roshan Sandor DeSol." His voice trailed off as his eyes flicked toward the door. He waved his hand at someone, which caught Faye's attention.

"She wanted to know if you're ready," was all the other male said, and impatiently so.

That was all he had to say, and at once Faye knew it was Jaran. "You have got to be kidding me. Jaran..." As if her voice could grow even quieter, it did just that. "Why were you in the marketplace, being arrested nonetheless?"

Roshan took the plate from her grasp and set it down on a nearby table. One of his hands took up hers, and he held it lightly. "There is evil afoot and forgive me for lying, but there are more than feelings at stake—there are countries on the brink of war."

"I know! Your father... is he here tonight?"

"No, I told him to remain home, and I came in his place. I was hoping to find you there. I had... a dream, it sounds weird, but it is the truth."

"Something wretched is going to happen tonight." She looked down at their hands and squeezed her eyes shut. "Zev wants to marry me and use me as a tool."

"A tool?" He sounded confused.

"I am Faye, the Lady of Alindor, and though you may not believe me, Nymiane has bound me to the mundane realm. She wishes to start a war with Alindor and Melothra, and I am powerless."

Roshan swallowed audibly and released her hands, one lifted to tilt her face up toward the moonlight. "I believe you, and perhaps I wouldn't if Etain hadn't visited me in my dreams, and if Jaran had not beaten it into my thick skull."

"Etain?" she whispered. Had her sister visited him? "How do you know Jaran?"

He pulled away from her and ran his fingers through his hair. "Yes, red hair… dramatic flair and flowing gown," he paused for a moment as if considering how much to reveal. "He's loyal to Alindor," was all he said. "Where is Zev?" Roshan's voice hardened.

"Occupied with Majidah."

"Good." He walked away from the railing and toward the door, peering inside. "Get the knight prepared," he ordered to Jaran and held out a hand to Faye. "The buns will have to wait, Faye, it's time to dance while your knight prepares."

"I don't think I can manage a dance," she protested.

Roshan grinned down at her as he led her to the dance floor. "We will make do just fine," he offered as he slid a hand along her back and threaded his fingers with hers.

Faye could not remember when the last time she danced had been. As they slid into position, she felt her cheeks burn, the proximity allowed her to smell the warm citrus musk that came from him.

"I will get you home, I promise." The vow slipped from him as he began to lead her around the room, their bodies subtly touching throughout the dance.

She trusted that he would at least try—all of them would—and when it came down to it, Faye would not let Nymiane prevail. "Why did your father hide you?" she asked, somewhat hypnotized by the way their bodies traversed the marble floor.

Lowering his voice even more, he dipped his head forward so he could offer the answer to her. "It was my choice so that none knew what I looked like and I could easily blend in with a crowd without anyone suspecting a thing. It makes for easy traveling—

at least it did until now." He chuckled and squeezed her hand before spinning her around.

Miraculously, she stumbled only a few times. Roshan guided her around the floor and graciously did not so much as make a noise when she stepped on his toes.

Once the dance was through, he cast a glance over the room. Faye did the same, not spotting Zev or Majidah's aura amongst the crowd. Bodies crowded the dance floor and poured out of the banquet hall. "He's still not here," she whispered.

"Time to get to the knight."

The process of hiding Faye was not an easy one. Apologizing profusely as he bent down, Roshan folded the dress in such a way so that it hugged her legs like men's pants. He had the decency to flush as much as Faye did. To better hide her features, a cloak was wrapped around her and the hood snugly fitted around her face.

"I'm sorry," he said for the umpteenth time.

"Well gods above, Roshan, you don't even have the decency to court her properly first?" Jaran teased, lips pulling back to reveal a flash of white teeth.

Sandor cast a glare in his direction and stood to his feet, his hand seeking Faye's out. "I apologized," he paused and turned to Faye. "I apologize... again."

"He's always putting his hands on you in some way, be careful," Jaran whispered and grunted as an elbow found his stomach.

Pressing her lips together, Faye held in a laugh and followed the two down the hall, what awaited them at the stairwell was not something she had anticipated.

"I'll meet you outside," Jaran stated before he branched off down the hallway and disappeared.

"Trust me, also... I apologize again..." Roshan whispered, his movements became unsteady, and his arm slid around her back. "Come outside with me, love," he slurred his words as he feigned being intoxicated. "It's too crowded inside..." His thick lashes lowered as he smiled cheekily at her.

Moving along with him, her hand reached up to tentatively

touch his chest, and she heard the sharp intake of his breath. His fingers flexed along her back which made butterflies take flight in her belly.

They moved down the stairs, noticed, but their presence didn't trigger alarms in the guards as they wound their way down. It wasn't an easy task, not when guards seemed to be at every twist and turn, but they made it to an awaiting carriage.

"Zola?" Faye asked Roshan.

"Not here, she went ahead, there were too many guards." He aided her into the cab and sat opposite of her, tapping on the roof.

The hood of the cloak fell, the mask gleaming in the moonlight. Faye let out a breath, her heart hammering.

"May I?" he asked softly.

"What?"

He leaned forward and carefully extracted the first mask from her face. "Maybe I'll keep it in memory of this night." He eyed it for a moment and laid it on his knee.

Something twisted inside of her chest, it wasn't as if they knew one another, but they had shared a few glorious moments together.

"Can I at least try?" He sounded unsure as his hand extended toward her.

"I don't know, what if..." She swallowed roughly and lifted the hood back into place.

Panic spread through her, causing her limbs to stiffen and as the carriage suddenly halted, she was sent forward enough so that their heads collided.

A hiss escaped Roshan as he rubbed his head. "I deserved that," he mumbled with a laugh. "Let me try, we are on our way, and we have a head start."

He didn't need to continue, Faye knew where he was going. They had a head start which meant Zev had little to no chance of finding them before they reached the border—as long as they didn't hit any roadblocks.

She said nothing, but she nodded her head and leaned forward to let him try.

Roshan's fingers solicitously ran along the seam of the mask, his thumb brushed along her cheekbone, and when he tugged at the porcelain, there was no fight. It slid free into his grasp which made him pull back quicker than he anticipated. His back hit the cushion behind him, and he laughed nervously. "It worked," he said breathlessly.

A gasp came from her, and her hands slid to her face which had not felt the air on it in months. Torn between laughing and crying, she leaned her face into her hands, reveling in the feeling.

With care, she lifted her head to peer up at Roshan, she did not want to chance the hood falling—after all, there was only one that could remove the mask, wasn't that the key?

Faye stared at him with her mouth agape. She wasn't sure what she had been expecting. His nose was pert, his skin only a few shades darker than hers made his green eyes stand out all the more. They were such a light hue of green, it gave him an ethereal appearance. His defined jaw had a faint coating of stubble on it, and his hair was a sandy shade of brown. Sandor —*Roshan*—was beautiful.

"Are you okay?" he finally asked.

Overwhelmed, but okay, she thought. Roshan didn't seem crazed or suddenly inspired to cause mayhem. "You're beautiful," she murmured.

He flushed all the way to the roots of his hair and lowered his eyes as he opened his mouth to speak. "Faye I—"

The carriage halted, and it began to rock as the driver moved around. He must have leaped from the front because the door opened. Moonlight spilled in, but the face remained hidden by shadows.

"Yer gonna have to get out here, the rider is waitin'."

She knew that voice, it didn't matter what his face looked like, and she leaped from her seat to hug him tightly. "Leon! How did you?... Oh, Zola," she said softly, confusion lacing her tone.

"Jaran and Zola," Roshan said slowly, "In the market—if you recall, they were relaying messages." His fingers toyed with the mask on his knee, his teeth snagging his upper lip. "She can fill you in on the rest. I should get back to the party before I'm accused of something." Half smiling, he folded his hands on his lap.

"Thank you, Sandor, I won't forget you."

"Oh, I won't forget you, not for a long time," he said with a laugh.

Leon tugged Faye from the confines of the cab and thumbed toward the waiting horse. Sitting astride the steel grey horse was Zola, with braided dark hair, and dark leather riding attire. She looked like a force to be reckoned with.

"Oh," Leon stammered as he set her down. "My Goddess..." he whispered breathlessly, unable to keep his eyes trained on her face.

"It's just me, Leon. Tell me that Jacob is alive," she began to say and found herself unable to continue.

"Aye, sweet goddess, he is alive and sends his regards."

The words warmed Faye to the core, but her eyes did not remain on Leon for long, for they flicked to Zola.

"Well, don't just gawk at me, get on before my father realizes you're missing. We have a half hour ride to Alindor, and more than that to get to the temple. He won't be able to make his announcement come midnight, and he's going to be rankled."

Faye staggered, and it wasn't from lack of sight, because that had been granted to her again, no—it was the truth. Zola was Zev's daughter?

"Yep, now you understand why I never wanted to see him again. I'm sorry, Faye, I wish I could have told you more."

"No, don't apologize, I withheld the truth from all of you. I knew who I was..." She moved toward Sarge and patted his shoulder fondly. This is why her dress had been tied around he legs.

"You're just as I Saw in my vision," Zola said in a softer tone. There was an anxious quality to her expression, but given the situation, it was understandable. "I will explain later, but now we must ride."

Leon boosted Faye up and on to Sarge, she shifted and wrapped her arms around Zola. "Take care of Prince Roshan—" Just as his name left her lips a loud explosion burst and lightning streamed across the sky. The horse spooked but remained in place, all of them peered toward the castle.

A curse flew from Roshan as he peered out of the carriage, his eyes darting toward the sky, toward the castle itself. "Majidah," he cursed as he leaped from the carriage. "Get Faye out of here!" he ordered.

"What do you mean, 'Majidah,'" Zola shouted.

"You need to get out of here, too. From the looks of it, Prince, you've already been found out, so you better go." Leon didn't need any prompting, he moved toward his horse and unhitched it. It wasn't Faith; she was stocky, while this horse was more akin to a racer. "I didn't come ill-prepared." He stripped the last of the harness off of the horse except for the bridle. "Both of you be gone—there are a lot of highwaymen out this way," he said with a wink.

Roshan's light green eyes slid toward Zola. "I mean, she had planned on attacking Zev—and my father. She's likely killed him, if not crippled him. Judging by the explosion, I daresay he's dead." He turned his gaze to Leon. "Thank you," Roshan offered and hopped up on the horse. "Let's go."

Roshan's expression tightened, he didn't look behind them again as they darted off on horseback, but he did glance over at them as he spoke. "I wasn't sure, but I had spread word that Majidah had a stake in this game, too. I don't think Zev took the message seriously, he had his weapon of choice..." His gaze slid to Faye meaningfully.

"What?" Zola snapped as she maneuvered the horse along the bridle path. "You couldn't have had Jaran pass that snippet along?"

Dread crept in, she felt her limbs grow cold, and her fingers dug into Zola. "It's not real," Faye murmured. "The curse—I mean, only in part, but you were supposed to take it off because she knew if you did..." The hood fell from her head as if on cue, realization dawned on all of them. If Alindor removed the mask, it would cause hysteria between the other two kingdoms, because they'd want what they had. They'd claw at one another, and they'd do everything to gain the upper hand.

"Damn you, Nymiane! It wasn't ever about the mask—it was about what she could make everyone think, and to create greed amongst them. Greed breeds chaos!"

A string of curses rang out from Zola, and Roshan sped his horse up and urged her to do the same. "There's going to be a war, and it'll be my head—Alindor's fault. All eyes will turn on Alindor."

"She's been too quiet," Faye murmured, her eyes darting upward. For the first time in two months, she saw the heavens. Velvet speckled with thousands of twinkling diamonds and hints of blue streaked across the sky. "I won't let Alindor take the fall," she said firmly.

"I suspect fun games are to be had soon," Roshan offered wryly. "As much as I'd love to believe it won't, it would be foolish not to plan accordingly."

The rest of their journey went quietly, it wasn't until they reached the border of Alindor did Roshan speak again.

"I'd say may the Lady of Light be with you, but..." he teased as they crossed over into Alindor, the sound of the horse's hooves pounding on the newly formed sheets of ice echoed in the forest.

"How charming," Zola remarked with a snort.

It was amusing and likely would have been more so if Faye didn't feel entirely useless. "Kathill isn't far from here at least." Which was a blessing because the horses were growing tired, their breaths were more labored, and the last thing that she wanted was for Sarge or Roshan's runner to fall victim to overexertion.

Overhead, a crow let out a cackle before it swept low, momentarily spooking the horses. It wasn't that which had a scream tearing from Faye, but an arrow had struck her side. No doubt it had been meant for the Prince of Alindor, but in the darkness, it had bit into her flesh instead.

"Faye!" cried Roshan, concern tightening his features.

Pain radiated in cold waves each time she was jostled by Sarge's large movements. "I'm fine," she called out to him. "Where did that—" A thunk in the tree cut her words off. Men were on their tailthey were onto them. Somehow, they had managed to catch up.

"Just ride!" Zola ordered and opted for a less traveled path.

Faye knew the land, she felt a dull hum as if it were trying to communicate with her, but without the restoration of her birthright, she would not be able to call it properly. "I wouldn't normally ask, Zola, but can you..."

Zola sucked in a breath before she began muttering something under it. "I should have surmised that you knew." One of her hands moved from her hold on the reins, she didn't look behind her, but as she conjured up energy in the palm of her hand, she released her hold on it. Light burst behind them, illuminating the dark figures on their horses.

None of the three looked behind them as the light erupted

and shook the earth. There would be more soon, and there was no time to spare.

"Faye, are you okay?" Roshan shouted.

Each jostling movement sucked the wind from her. The blood oozing from the wound began to feel cold, it was sticky as well. "I will be." It would have to be good enough.

The horses bolted from the woods onto a beaten path that led into the city of Kathill. Their hooves sounded distant to Faye, she could have sworn she heard Etain's voice shrieking her name, and it was enough to jolt her fully awake.

In the distance, Faye saw the castle—it was close to midnight, but the building nearly glowed under the pale light. She knew that the temple wasn't too far from the castle and as she swept her gaze along the way, she caught sight of it.

"It was like someone lobbed a boulder from the sky, but nothing was there. The ceiling collapsed onto the floor, and a fire broke out in the Kathill Temple during a mass," Roshan supplied. His light eyes flicked to the arrow jutting out of Faye's side and he grit his teeth, pulling his mount up short. "I need to get to the castle to alert them. I will ride to the temple with you, but then I must go."

Zola nodded her head. "Maybe you should—"

"I said I'd ride to the temple," he cut her off.

Faye pulled the cloak from her, growing uncomfortable with the extra fabric around her and discarded it. "Just get me there." She sounded short, but they rode off.

She all but fell off Sarge as they made it there.

Roshan rushed to her side, his arms carefully lifting her up. "Gods above, Faye you're soaked in blood!" He didn't bother to move his hand away.

Faye moved her head so that she could look up at him without leaning backward. The moon bathed his warm complexion; even though it was tight with frustration and worry, he was beautiful.

One of his hands lifted to brush the hair away from her face, and he shook his head. "Go, I can't stay, go." Something akin to regret flashed in his gaze before he turned away and mounted his horse again.

Something glinted at the bottom of the steps, the blue and silver mask lay discarded. Zola considered it for a moment and then began to rush up the stairs with Faye by her side.

By the time they reached the inside, Faye had collapsed to her knees and began to crawl toward the altar. She batted away Zola's hands, grimacing through the pain as she pulled herself onto it.

Her hand moved to feel for the arrow, and she yanked the shaft which made her cry out. Hot blood spilled from her wound and onto the altar, it was funny—she was essentially a sacrifice in her own temple.

Coughing, she felt liquid seep between her lips and saw specks of blood on the marble altar. It hadn't occurred to her that she would die a mortal's death, but hadn't her sister promised as much? She could have sworn she heard Zola scream, but the light faded from her vision, and she was soon tumbling into a starry sky.

When she opened her eyes again, she saw a blur of red hair, and it took her a moment to process the sharp features and the wide-set green eyes.

Etain.

Etain's hand cupped Faye's cheek, and she pointed to her side. She had healed her; in its place was a bruise. "I am so sorry, Faye, please, believe me, I didn't know that she'd go this far… and when I protested, she held me captive. Believe me."

As much as Faye wanted to shake her sister, she did believe her. Wiping her eyes, she refocused them and looked around—it was her home. She was in her bed of down, and there was a bowl of blood off to the side—her blood.

Looking down, she took note of the white dress she wore. "Where is she?"

"She's indisposed at the moment. Kaja, the blacksmith, imbued his chains with some of your reflection pool's water, it will hold her, but not for long."

A laugh escaped Faye, the pure water would keep her at bay until they tested whether or not her power could be restored to her. "Serves her right," she muttered.

Etain helped her from the bed and led her out of the room.

The house was not unlike the temple or castle of Kathill, it was of gold and ivory. The floor was crafted of marble and had streaks of gold inlaid in it as well. Sculptures of the old gods littered small shelves in the hall which gave it a mundane feeling.

"Hurry," Etain offered as she rounded a corner to the reflection pool room. If the other rooms were light, this one was brilliant. Skylights shone down onto the pool reflecting the bright sky above.

"Don't you dare!" Nymiane shouted as she ran forward, hand reaching out to grab at Faye's hair.

Etain stopped her and threw her into a wall. "Get in the pool!" Her head snapped to the side as Nymiane shoved it.

Faye didn't waste any time, she ran toward the pool and dove into the depths. The rush of water brushed passed her, the ache in her side protested, but as she swam through the warm water, she felt revitalized, felt energy she hadn't been connected to in months course through her once more.

The pool illuminated, and a rush of water burst from it as Faye climbed out. Whereas her skin had been porcelain before, it seemed to glow, her light eyes flicked toward Nymiane who was charging forward.

"No, you're in my home, my land!" Faye shouted. Nymiane's claws raked against her cheek, drawing blood. She splayed her hands against her shoulders and pushed her back.

"It doesn't matter, you're too late." A wicked grin tugged at her lips as she regained her footing. "Melothra's king is dead; Nedrand will move in, and Alindor's Prince fled during the ball… highly suspect if you ask me."

"So it's true? Zev is dead?" Faye questioned, although it had been assumed this was the first confirmation.

"Yes, Majidah didn't take much coaxing from her patron goddess, she's a wicked darling. She dreamed it up months ago, with my help of course, and it was why she and Zev were bedmates. She knew one day she'd gut him, and that was just what she did." Nymiane twisted her hand as if it held a knife.

This was enough. Faye backhanded Nymiane. It wasn't too late—it was never too late—it would take some doing, but this could be fixed. "You tried to have me killed, you sent me there to rot and to inspire a war across the continent!" Thunder rolled, and even in the land of the light, the skies began to darken.

Nymiane shrank, her eyes filling with worry. "What have you done?"

"What could I do? I've done nothing, this is all on you, and it is time you pay for your sins."

Whipping her head to the side, Nymiane gawked at Etain, her bottom lip trembling as she gathered her skirt. "You didn't…"

"You left me no choice, your greed has gotten the best of you." Etain lowered her gaze and stepped to the side as a fleet of guardians flocked into the room. They were clad in gold and lined up against the wall. As the next individual came into the room, they took a knee.

"Father," Faye said softly, disbelief entering her voice.

"Bind her," Akos motioned toward Nymiane, disgust etched in every line on his face. "Don't fuss, I have no patience for your antics right now." His attention turned toward Faye once more as he moved toward her, his arms stretching out. "Etain sent word as soon as she could."

Not wasting a moment, Faye entered her father's embrace, but she didn't linger there, she turned to face her wicked sister. "What will her punishment be?"

"A few centuries in the Underworld aiding Katahn might do her some good."

"No!" Nymiane hissed. "Bind me to a desert, put me to sleep for a few centuries."

Akos pinned her with a glare. "So you can find a way to escape? No, Katahn will employ you, and there is no way you'll manage to escape him." With a flick of his hand his retinue bound her and carted her off, she didn't leave without a fight.

Chapter 13

Etain confessed her part in the plan; she had wanted more patrons worshipping her, her sister had convinced her if Faye was out of the picture, that they could split Alindor. Of course, that was far from the plan.

"I didn't think she would go this far, I'm sorry Faye, truly." Etain had the good graces to lower her head into her hands to weep.

Akos sighed, his hand running down his face. "Your sentence will be lightened, but you will not be skipping out on a punishment." He thumbed the door and turned to his daughter. "Now about this temple," he began, waving his hand to gaze into the pool.

In the depths of the water, Faye could see her discarded dress and a pool of blood on the altar, Zola was clutching the fabric in her hands in a fit of tears. It occurred to Faye this was what she had seen in her vision weeks ago, she knew it was coming, and perhaps that was precisely why she had distanced herself.

"It needs to be repaired, as does the land. Nymiane's disease began to spread." Frustrated she turned away from the pool and glowered. "Not all of it can be undone."

Akos let loose a breath and sat down along the pool's edge and pat it. "Just as a fire cleanses the land, sometimes change does, too."

She moved to the pool and sat down, her father's fingers tugging her hair away from her face. "Peace, little one, show them why they should believe in their Lady. It's been a long time since one of us walked amongst mankind. Maybe we'd all benefit from that motion." He leaned forward and brushed his lips to her brow and stood to his feet.

Father was right, and so she pulled back the veil to the other realm and let her body take form inside the temple. Immediately, her ears were met with the sound of sobbing, and she quickly made her way to Zola's side.

"You did well, Zola, you did well." Her hands ran along her back to soothe her, it startled her at first.

"You're alive," she whispered and swiped at her tears. "I thought you had died, you had vanished… the clock struck midnight, and you were gone."

"Zola, your father is dead," she began softly, "Melothra needs a leader, and since you're his only blood, they need you." It was a lot to take in. Faye also knew there was no love for her father. She flinched—Faye could only assume it was the mention of taking to the throne, not the mention of his death.

"I don't know," was all that she mumbled.

"There is still some time to think about that, as for now… come." She stood to her feet and motioned for her to rise as well. Looking to the heavens, she lifted a hand, and with it, the rubble shifted; every piece that had broken apart during the blow moved into place, locking once more. In a few moments, the temple was restored.

"Our work is not through." Walking up to Sarge, her fingers touched upon his cheek. "You've been a good boy," she said softly, letting the renewed energy flow into his being. "We need to ride to the castle."

So they did.

Zola had warned her about the guards, that she just couldn't waltz into the courtyard without being announced and Faye shot her a glance over her shoulder. "I doubt that," she offered with a smile.

Dismounting from Sarge, Faye began on the steps, not one single guard questioned her presence, but they did drop to their knees, and she allowed it. As they ascended the last of the stairs, the door opened. Faye had not anticipated what she'd say upon entering, but as she rounded a corner, she caught the familiar profile of Sandor—Roshan.

"You missed all the action," Zola teased.

"I think he's glad for it," Faye murmured.

Spinning around to face them, he looked startled at first and then relaxed before he strode forward. "What? How did…" His words trailed off as he took in Faye's appearance. "My Lady," he whispered softly.

"She died in the temple," Zola began, her voice cracking from the memory.

"No," Faye interrupted and lifted her hands when she saw the look on his face. "Almost, but I didn't. Did they believe you—are they making preparations?"

Roshan nodded grimly. "We will go to war, Nedrand will settle easily, but Melothra is another thing."

"Zev has died, and it is without a ruler for the moment," Faye said and did not so much as glance at her friend.

"I suspected as much. We will do what we can to prevent senseless bloodshed, but there is no other way." He sighed heavily as he approached her. He lifted a hand as if he wanted to touch her face but pulled back last minute, thinking better of it.

"I will give you two a moment," Zola said, not waiting for the dismissal she moved out down the hallway.

"I cannot stay, I'll only cause more disruptions," she began and watched as he dropped his hands. A part of her yearned to feel the warmth of them against her face. "But I wanted to thank you. As such, your country will gain blessings for remaining true, and your neighbors who remained faithful, too." She moved forward and took up one of his hands, lifting it so she could feel it against her skin."Be safe, and I promise I will be with you. You kept your promise, and I will keep mine."

Roshan let loose a breath, his green eyes peering into hers as his thumb brushed against her cheek. "You're remarkable," he whispered softly.

Faye's lips tugged into a smile, and she decided at that moment, in spite of everything, that she wanted more than anything to kiss him. She tilted her head up and caught his breath against her lips, their eyes locked, and she felt his fingers slip into her hair. Roshan met her halfway and tentatively kissed her. He was careful at first and then deepened it.

Gods above, this was wonderful! She felt her body sigh into his and was more than eager to return the kiss. Boldly, her arms draped around his shoulders and she allowed for her body to mold against his. She felt his muscled shoulders tense, and felt more than her desire mounting—she felt his,too.

Roshan's fingers combed through her hair and slid beneath

her chin so that he could gain better access to her mouth. A groan escaped him as he savored the kiss.

It was wonderful, this was what it felt like to be kissed? Faye mused, but lost herself in the moment. It wasn't until a throat cleared behind them that she pulled away.

"Always," Jaran began, "You always have your hands on her. You need to work on your courting skills, Prince Not-So-Charming." He had a grin on his face, beside him Zola shook her head.

"Don't listen to him, take your time, Faye, I'll keep him occupied," Zola teased and pinched Jaran's arm.

"Oh…" Jaran grinned wickedly at her and dipped his head to steal a kiss. "Lead the way, lover." He followed after her, pointedly wiggling his bottom like a dog following its master.

Roshan let out a chuckle, his fingers slipping away from Faye's hair and she saw the sudden change in his gaze, it went from absolute bliss to sadness.

"We never did get to eat our sticky buns," he said softly.

It wasn't goodbye, was it? She felt her heart twist and opened her mouth to contradict that notion, but was it? "Soon," she said, "soon we'll have those sticky buns. Jaran said you needed to court me, and I agree. I've never had one court me before." As she pressed her lips together, she lowered her head and felt her cheeks flush with color.

His fingers slid beneath her chin, and he gently tilted her head back, a friendly grin on his face. "Then that is precisely what I'll do, name the day and I'll come with an entire platter full of sticky buns."

She leaned forward, lifting her eyebrows playfully. "Every full moon at midnight?"

"Your house or mine?" He inched forward, his gaze locked on hers.

"Mine. If you offer those sticky buns, I will come." A laugh escaped her. Mid-laugh she felt his lips brushing hers and shyly she buried her head into his neck.

"I will." He buried his nose into her hair and smiled.

"I will come to you, too."

"Promise?" he whispered softly, searching her eyes.

"I promise." She turned her head to press a soft kiss to his lips.

Roshan's fingers teased the back of her neck, and just as he was readying to kiss her back, she allowed herself to fade from the mundane realm. He didn't need her as a distraction, and though they had both made a promise to one another, she had work to do in her kingdom and him in his.

Twelve moonlit midnights passed since the events in Melothra took place. The first month after was taxing. Faye had to watch as war swept through the lands, but she held her promise and blessed her followers, had blessed the land below, too. Still, she held her breath and counted the days until the moon would once again be full.

Of course, her time was full of repairing her realm, too. Etain had been removed from ruling Melothra, and with Nymiane bound in the netherworld, two vacancies had to be filled. Akos sent his brothers Nam and Skor to rule in the meantime. Zola had also fought for her right to rule and had in the recent months became Queen of Melothra, and had a hand in de-throning Majidah, which allowed for her daughter Kira to come into power.

However, the moment the clock struck midnight Faye whisked herself away to the human realm. Immediately, her senses were tickled by the scent of sticky buns. Roshan knelt at the altar with a platter of them, his head bowed and a beautiful smile on his lips.

"Let me see your face," she ordered as she stepped closer. Today was extra special, it was Sandor's nineteenth birthday, he no doubt had spent most of the evening partying.

Roshan lifted his head so that he could look up at her.

Her heart hammered in her chest as she moved down the steps to meet him. "Sandor," she whispered and reached her hand out to cup his face. He caught it between his hands, and she felt his lips brush her soft skin.

"No more of this, please," he begged her. "No more, I beg of you." His head bowed over her hand again.

A spear of pain pierced her heart—he was human, and more than that, he was the heir to the throne of Alindor. Instead of pulling away, she pushed the plate of pastries aside and sat before him, her arms encircling his shoulders so she could pull him to her chest.

"What of Alindor, my love?" She brushed her lips to his forehead.

"What of it?" he asked wryly and pulled back. "Didn't you hear? My father's new wife had a son." It sounded pitiful as he spoke as if he knew the answer.

But he didn't, apparently. "Oh," Faye said quietly, her fingers stroking along his jawline as he pulled his gaze away from her. "Sandor..." she said his name softly.

"I love you, and each moon phase, I love you more..."

Perhaps it was a human thing to overthink things, perhaps he was rubbing off on her, but Faye quickly leaped to the worst. "But you don't want to do this anymore."

His eyes widened, and he quickly gathered her hands in his grasp. "No, no, dammit," he muttered the last under his breath as he let a frustrated breath out. "I want to be your husband, Faye. I don't want an entire month between each moment I see you," he began, his fingers pulling away from her hand so he could tuck her hair behind her ear. "I want to rise with you, I want to be there when you close your eyes at night. To the end of time, Faye."

What could she say to that? Words failed her, and perhaps she should have encouraged him to remain here, to serve the kingdom as a good prince, and one day king. The world needed more people like him, yet she found herself being utterly selfish at that moment, too. She wanted him as a husband.

"And if you should deny me, I'll have you know, I'll look like the biggest fool. I already told everyone goodbye, and my brother was named the new heir this evening. I clearly had a lot of faith in my ability to talk."

"Sandor..."

He didn't cease talking though. "Which I'm clearly failing at and for that, I—" His words met their end as Faye shoved a sticky bun in his mouth. He bit down on it and eyed her quizzically.

Leaning forward, she pulled it back and pressed her lips

against his. She tasted the honey and spices there. "Yes, I accept your proposal."

He swallowed roughly. The breath he had been holding whooshed out with a laugh, his arms encircled Faye as he peppered kisses on her lips and face. "Then… we go home?"

Home. He referred to her realm as home. "Yes, we go home."

ACKNOWLEDGMENTS

I sincerely want to thank you, the reader, for taking the time to read Faye's story.

This particular tale has been with me since 2004, and it's been itching to be released. Faye was definitely tired of living in the shadows that Nymiane insisted she remained in!

This is only the beginning of a journey for me, one that has taken a while for me to work the nerve up to begin! So stay tuned for some more pent-up stories from me.

A huge thank you to my #writingsquad! Lou and Christis. You girls have allowed me to hone my craft throughout our years together. Thank you for that, and thank you for listening to me fret over whether or not my stories were good enough.

K.M. I wouldn't be here if you didn't yank me from my turtle shell. Also, this book cover is by K.M., and without her talents, this would be a sad, naked book. [No one wants to see that!]

Thank you, Jess, for helping me with this story, and Yentl for being there and always being excited for me no matter what, valkyries for life!

My entire family for encouraging my writing and never outwardly [possibly inwardly,] rolling their eyes and calling me crazy for my strange ideas—and also the mornings I'd wake up rambling last night's bizarre dream.

My brother, Zachary, those writing sessions in my room

while listening to Evanescence meant more to me than what you'll ever realize.

Most of all I want to thank my mother, for taking me to bookstores, reading me bedtime stories, and encouraging my wild imagination. I know my creativity comes from you and my desire to devour books at an alarming rate. So thank you for supporting me in all things—but especially my writing. I'll love you forever, I'll like you for always.

VEILED ALLUREMENT PLAYLIST

Music is a huge part of my writing, as such, I'd like to offer you the opportunity to listen to the music that inspired a lot of moments in this book. Feel free to look me up on Spotify [Elle Beaumont,] but below is the soundtrack!

•Let's Hurt Tonight by OneRepublic
•When You Come Back Down by Kina Grannis
•Hard To Do by Gavin James
•Dance With Me To The End of Love by The Civil Wars
•The Wreck of Our Hearts by Sleeping Wolf
•Everybody Knows by Sigrid

ABOUT AUTHOR

Elle was born and raised in Southeastern, Massachusetts in a little farm town by the harbor. She grew up fascinated with all things whimsical and a strong love for animals. As she grew, so did her passion for reading and writing. Although she prefers devouring all genres, she largely enjoys dark fantasy.

www.ellebeaumontbooks.com
facebook.com/ellebeaumontbooks
instagram.com/ellebeaumontbooks
twitter.com/ellebeaumont

ALSO BY ELLE BEAUMONT

Brotherhood of the Sea
Binding of the Sea

BROTHERHOOD OF THE SEA

Eighteen-year-old Jagger and his older brother, Kriegen, are recent graduates from Selith Academy—an elite school for Merfolk. The two work to help their community after tragedy befell their father, but when the Uplanders break a promise, the two mermen only have one goal—keep the Merfolk safe at any cost.

When the brothers are divided in their responses, they quickly learn that every choice has a consequence, and every action has a price.

How far is too far when it comes to sacrifice under the sea?

BINDING OF THE SEA

Selith Academy trains elite Merfolk in perfecting their magical abilities, hosting a Trial every twelve years. When Zinnia—one of their most gifted students—and her friend, Dru witness Prince Loch threatening an infamous Sea Witch for his magical abilities despite the royal family hosting the upcoming Trial, they start an investigation that will uncover buried truths and jeopardize the entire kingdom.

Zinnia and Dru will find help from an unexpected source as they use their magic to help bind evil back into the depths when they find themselves at the forefront of the battle that has surfaced after four centuries.

Will the sea's buried truth destroy them all?

www.ingramcontent.com/pod-product-compliance
Lightning Source LLC
Chambersburg PA
CBHW032020180726
48283CB00008B/2770